I0521316

SHIELDING SHAYNA

BROTHERHOOD PROTECTORS WORLD

HEATHER LONG

Twisted Page Press LLC

Copyright © 2018 by Twisted Page Press, LLC

All rights reserved.

This work was made possible through a special license through
Twisted Page Press LLC and has not been reviewed by Twisted
Page Press LLC. All scenes, events, plots, characters and related
elements appearing in the original Brotherhood Protectors series
remain the exclusive copyrighted and/or trademarked property of
Twisted Page Inc., or there affiliates or licensors.

No part of this book may be reproduced in any form or by any
electronic or mechanical means, including information storage and
retrieval systems, without written permission from the author,
except for the use of brief quotations in a book review.

BROTHERHOOD PROTECTORS

ORIGINAL SERIES BY ELLE JAMES

SERIES SO FAR

SHIELDING SHAYNA

Honor comes in all sizes.

Shayna Morgan has been a little bit of everything in her life—a daughter, a niece, a sailor, an investigator, and homeless. Nerve damage has left her with only partial feeling on her right side, and pain threatened to cripple her. Family pulled her home from where she slept in her car outside of DC, but it was the men and women of the Brotherhood Protectors who inspired her and gave her a purpose. She may not be able to fire a gun with any accuracy, but her new project fulfills her in so many other ways—helping other female vets just like her. It's all hard, honest work and good sweat until a shadowy threat takes aim at her ranch.

Purpose comes in all shapes.

Fergus "Oddjob" Roper went into the Air Force at 18, before making a lateral move to the Navy, and then left the SEALs when he was 33. After 15 years of service, two wars, multiple deployments and 3 degrees, he's looking for his next mission. After a year in Texas working with a horse trainer specializing in equine support animals, he's heading to Montana to visit with old friends. He came for the beer, and stayed for the women...one woman in particular. Oddjob doesn't mind mucking stalls, or helping out on the project—but what he wants is to shield the woman who saved his life, even if she doesn't know it.

Danger doesn't always take a direct approach, but Oddjob plans to have Shayna's back as she gets ready to tangle with a whole new kind of enemy.

NOTE FROM THE AUTHOR

As always, thank you Elle James for letting me play with your characters. I have so much fun visiting Montana in these books I want to take a trip for real each time! Also, dear readers, some of the characters appearing here have shown up in previous installments. Sometimes, these guys just want to play their part. Every hero is different and the same can be said of the women they meet. How they overcome the challenges facing them, that's the important part.

xoxo

Heather

CHAPTER 1

LIFE HAPPENS whether you're ready for it or not, but that was why I came to Celebrate—and why I stayed. Celebrate is here to help women who served and sacrificed for this great nation when life threw them an unexpected curve ball. Shayna Morgan recited her mantra internally as she made her way from the house to the barn. The ranch—Celebrate—was coming together. It wasn't Brighter Days, and the mission more specifically focused, yet none of it would be possible if not for Brighter Days and the Brotherhood Protectors.

Speaking of the Brotherhood, the man standing at the corral brushing Ace cast a smile in her direction. The rugged former SEAL with his dark beard and thick dark hair possessed a casual air belying his serious skills and background. Hank Patterson recommended him and after a full assessment of the letters she'd received coupled with some unlikely accidents on the property she was trying to get into shape.

"Good morning Oddjob," she said, unabashedly loving Fergus Roper's nickname. When Hank mentioned him after their meeting, she'd pictured a brash Irishman with ginger hair and freckles, not the strapping dark haired man with sun-kissed skin and enigmatic dark green eyes. Nothing about him was Irish, at least not on the surface, but his jacket included stints in both the Air Force and the Navy. The man was a little bit of everything.

More. The horses loved him.

Ace in particular leaned into him as he continued to run the soft rubber brush along the horse's sides.

"Good morning, Shayna." A flash of a smile teased her, but it was the way he said her name that riveted her. He'd only been on the property twenty-four hours and she delighted in his company. "How are you today?" Though his gaze didn't dip to her right leg, she didn't doubt he'd noticed her limp. No matter how much she stretched or used a combination of heat and ice—it took a while each morning to get up and move. Within an hour or so, the limp would be barely noticeable and if she didn't push it—she wouldn't be limping at all by lunch.

"A little embarrassed you beat me out to the barn." Granted his apartment was located above the barn— an apartment she'd recently vacated after the work on the main house had been finished. She currently had eight rooms available, each with two—sometimes four beds for those with bunks, for incoming veterans and their families. The work on the cabins spread across the property would begin the following week.

"I couldn't sleep," he replied, seemingly unabashed. "This monster demanded attention as soon as I stepped out with my coffee." He motioned to a steaming cup sitting on the picnic table. "Help yourself, I can run upstairs and grab more."

She'd love to, but she'd just taken her first meds of the morning and they required at least thirty minutes to an hour to digest before she could eat or drink anything. "In a bit, but thank you." Tingles spread through her right hand as she flexed her fingers. Her shoulder ached and the arm itself flirted with fiery sparks along the nerve endings. "Don't spoil Ace too much." She started toward the barn, then hesitated. "Did the other horses demand breakfast too?"

Hints of a sheepish smile quirked Oddjob's lips as he circled Ace to continue grooming him on the side nearest her. The horse in question reached his head out toward her, and she accepted the demand to run her fingers gently over what had to be a velvety nose. She would be able to enjoy the sensation with her left hand, but it was good practice for her to watch what her right hand did because the feeling in it came and went. The tingles spread even more rapidly with every action.

Some days it turned from pins and needles to actual lances of fire and other days it went dead, like she wielded some flesh and bone prosthetic. If she allowed herself to dwell on it for too long, it would

3

depress the hell out of her. Had in fact—before the team found her and gave her a place here.

Shaking off the melancholy, she focused on Oddjob. "Thank you for feeding the horses, but that's not necessarily your job."

"No, and I appreciate that. I wanted to get a feel for the regular tasks of the day—and you had a chart posted on the feed room's whiteboard." It was not an apology, nor did she require one. "I also rode the perimeter last night and refueled the ATV after I got back."

She'd heard him go out. "What did you find?"

"It's wide open land, beautiful and isolated. You border three other ranches at various points and you've got good fence lines, but not everywhere."

Hard to fence it in fully. The wild life still needed a way through and she had horses—not cattle. At least not yet. "But no signs of vandalism?"

The issues at Celebrate began with simple vandalism—fence posts pulled out of the ground, a water tank turned blue with food coloring as it turned out—but they'd still had to drain it. Then someone else had taken a drill to every bucket—the holes so large they wouldn't carry water or grain. High school pranks, maybe. But Hank hadn't liked what he'd heard after the first accident—the brakes on her jeep had gone out and if she'd been going any faster or on one of the mountain roads, Shayna could have ended up in a fierce accident rather than just parked in a ditch.

The next accident involved her horses and that was when she'd called Hank. Hating to ask for help wasn't the same as being too stupid to seek it. Currently, Celebrate was a one woman operation with assistance, but they had to be ready to open their doors in just six weeks and she was ten weeks behind.

"None that I noticed. I'll do another pass after we get done with today's chores."

"Oddjob..." She almost sighed. When he arrived the day before she'd asked what he preferred to be called and he told her to pick. The nickname suited him, so she went with it. He'd finished grooming Ace and turned the gelding out to the paddock which had gone green with summer grass before returning to her and the picnic table.

"Yes?" The twinkle in his eyes arrested the unsettled feeling bubbling in her gut.

"Hank insisted I bring you on for protection." The need grated. Three years before, she wouldn't have any trouble handling her own protection—then the accident. She flexed her right hand again, ignoring the buzzing sensation which jolted from her fingertips to her shoulder before rebounding once more.

"I'll try not to overstep," Oddjob said as he settled on the edge of the table and claimed his coffee cup. "You sure you don't want a cup? I can grab you one from upstairs."

"Appreciate it, but I can't yet." Another sigh ripped from her. "Fuck, I feel like a bitch for even suggesting you're overstepping."

"On the contrary, you're in charge here and I'll take my lead from you in everything except your personal safety." Ease flowed through his tone. "That said, I just spent the last six months working a ranch in Texas, training with a Brit whose a damn gift with horses."

"Hank mentioned that...she specializes in PTSD animals, and therapy horses." Not that Celebrate would be specifically focusing on therapy, but rather providing resource based location to let female veterans get on their feet. It all sounded better in her head than on paper, but she was working on it. Residents would also have access to Brighter Days Ranch for more specific needs.

"Thought it sounded like a useful skill to have and I like horses better than most people." The man had a kind of gentle demeanor, easy to talk to, easy to trust —the horses probably adored him.

"I'd never even been on a horse before last year." But she'd fallen in love with them. "They're part of my therapy."

Stretching her right arm up across her chest, she used her left to press on the elbow and force the shoulder to stretch. The moves helped to loosen up the stiffness.

"How is that going?" His conversational tone expressed interest without demanding secrets.

"As well as can be expected, I'll never be 100 percent, not again." No, that transport left the base sometime between the bullet shattering the bad plate in her body armor and the slivers of shrapnel digging into her back. The torn muscle damage would have been enough, but the swelling of her spinal cord left her with souvenirs she'd never be able to return.

Pushing away from the abyss, she mentally back stepped. If she ventured too close to that hole, she'd tumble right back into the arms of bleak depression that not even alcohol could help her escape.

"Benchmarks are what we make them. We gotta define normal by what it means to us, not some average scale." With a shrug, he tipped his mug up for another drink even as he scanned the area. She'd bet real money he didn't miss much. Vigilance was an acquired skill, one she'd shared for many years particularly during her assignment as a FET—female engagement team—officer to deployed teams in Afghanistan and Iraq. Sometimes you only had a split second to respond to a niggling feeling.

"I know what I used to consider normal," she confessed, refusing the need to turn and scan the area herself. Instead she shifted her attention to the barn. The locals held a party eight weeks earlier when they'd all shown up to lend a hand and turn what had been a ramshackle structure into a solid barn, with an apartment upstairs, and get it wired for power and running pipes for water. She had only spent one winter in Eagle Rock so far, but after that experience, she wanted to be ready for anything.

Particularly if they got snowed in up here.

Of course, that's what the snowmobiles are for.

"The goal I have for this place is not only to define that new normal, but to build in a support network to grow achievement. I haven't achieved the normal I want—not yet."

"Sounds like a plan." A breeze stirred around them,

carrying hints of nature and fresh air. Earthier scents were welcome, a definitive difference from sand, cordite and blood she'd acclimated to in the Middle East or even the exhaust, pollution, and combination of food smells where she used to park her car back in D.C. when she'd had to sleep out of it. "What can I do to help?"

"You're already doing it—you're here." A part of her thought she should resent his presence, but she couldn't. If she wanted Celebrate to succeed, and she really did, then she needed someone more physically able than herself to make sure they made it to the finish line. "I need to walk." The ache in her hip had worked down to her thigh. "Care to join me? I can show you around."

They hadn't really had time for a tour the day before, and Hank had focused him more on defense. The rest of the Brotherhood Protectors would be making sporadic and unscheduled visits. If they kept the pattern erratic, the hope was to catch whomever was messing with the property.

For once, she hoped it was errant teenagers. They could scare them straight. If it was someone else... well, they'd deal with that battlefield when they got to it.

"I'd love to...give me a sec." He carried his coffee cup up the stairs next to the barn and disappeared inside. The apartment was great. She'd actually enjoyed the oversized studio feel of it, and the cozy nature of being right above the horses. The stairs, however, had sucked.

Another reason she'd moved into the main house as soon as it was ready. She had a bedroom on the first floor, tucked behind a room that would eventually become her office. Alone, she performed a deeper stretch and let out the grimace when her arm cramped before the stretch forced it to relax. Her meds only alleviated some of the symptoms—not the causes.

Fortunately, she'd been able to step down off the oxy for pain. While it let her relax, it also left her brain foggy and worse—it didn't get rid of all the pain. Nothing got rid of nerve pain. It just made her not care she suffered.

The sun warmed her back and she tilted her chin up to let the sun play across her face. The heat here was different than it was in D.C. or Afghanistan or just about anywhere she'd been. Growing up in the south where summer could be brutal, she'd thought herself prepared for Baghdad, Kandahar or even Abuja...but the sun was different in every place she'd ever served. The way the air tasted. The way the heat sank flaming claws into the body, and wrenched from it every drop of sweat.

Here, the heat was a blanket—a warm, comforting blanket. A kiss of respite from winter. She wasn't sure she'd ever be prepared for the way the snow insulated everything, and silenced the chorus of nature calls—birds, animals, and the breeze. Because even the wind sounded different.

"Here, I grabbed one for you too." Oddjob's voice

so close to her sent a jolt which jerked her out of her reverie. When the hell had he gotten back?

Failing to cover her surprise, she pivoted to find him holding a pair of portable lidded coffee mugs. Her heart hammered with the sudden dump of adrenaline and she had to force deeper breaths to unlock the muscles which stiffened across her shoulders.

"Sorry," he said with a wince. "Thought you heard me."

She should have. That kind of a distraction could get a Marine killed, but instead she'd been caught up admiring the damn sun. *New normal sucks.* "That's part of why you're here." Ego or not, honesty would get them farther on the road to figuring out what was going on. "I've been on property pretty regularly since we moved four horses over from Brighter Days. Which means I had to be here when they drilled those holes and I never heard them." Talk about embarrassing. Had she slept through their arrival? Through the use of equipment? Worse, she'd failed to notice anyone messing with the jeep, a vehicle that had also been on the property with her before it ended up in the ditch near the main road. A guy from town had picked it up and taken it in for repairs, in the meanwhile, Hank and his guys had been taking turns giving her rides.

Another reason to cut off the pain medication. Being dependent on anyone or anything didn't sit well with her. She liked being in control of her life, and her transport. Once upon a time, she'd been a light sleeper. Not true anymore.

"Anyway," she said, accepting the mug and motioning to the trail. "I've got focus issues. That's fine…that's on me. But I can't afford for anything to sabotage this project because of all the people who are counting on me, who trusted me to make this work, and for all the people it can help."

"Tell me a little more about that," Oddjob suggested as he fell into step with her. up close, he was even taller than he looked next to the horse. She wasn't a short woman, at 5'9, she could look most men in the eye. He easily had a head and then some on her. He had shoulders like a linebacker, and thick chest. If she were the person to have given him a nickname, she would have gone with Bear. Or Grizzly considering the facial hair.

"The accidents?" What did he want to know more about?

"This place." He took a sip of coffee and motioned to the ranch around them as they followed one of the paddock fences. With only four horses, she kept them all close. In addition to Ace, they had Goldie, Red, and Badass. The last horse had been one she'd grown to adore at Brighter Days, and they'd let her bring the mare with her. She was also the horse Shayna had regained some measure of her independence on.

"It's called Celebrate—the ranch, the land—and what buildings there are, were all donated by Jacob Dalton. Heard of him?" She hadn't before he'd made the pitch and Hank and his team offered her the job.

"He's—an actor. Used to be Special Forces." Of

course, Oddjob had heard of him. "Retired for a while now."

"Yeah, his daughter was a Marine. As it turns out, so was his mother. Go figure." They reached the first line of trees, demarcating where the land dropped away on a gentle slope. Pausing there, Shayna allowed herself a breather and then checked her watch. It had been more than thirty minutes, so she took a sip of the coffee. It was like magic in a cup, strong and dark. Perfection.

"Was." Her companion locked onto the verb.

"Yeah," Shayna said slowly, lowering the mug. "She committed suicide three years ago after battling an opiate addiction and PTSD. I didn't know her...but I knew her." She'd known a lot of veterans in similar straights. It was the dark underbelly of survival—the guilt, the flashbacks, and the cold emptiness of the soul. "He bought this place—I guess as a way to get out of Hollywood back in the day. Retreated up here when he needed a break. When I pitched the idea of a facility for female veterans, to help get them on their feet—he offered to back it. This property was the first donation."

"How did he even know—Hank." It wasn't a question.

"Actually Sadie, but close enough. She and Hank both knew him from his time here and they knew his story and what happened to his daughter. He came out to Brighter Days to volunteer from time to time, and that's how I met him." She liked the old guy. He was—real. Which seemed an odd description, but after meeting him she'd checked out his movies. "Have you ever seen his films?"

Oddjob laughed. "The one man army, he can kill something with a pair of toenail clippers?"

"Yeah," she said with a grin, then took another sip of the coffee. It was perfect. They'd started walking again. Every step loosened up the tautness in her joints. "I watched a marathon of them over the holidays. The funny thing is, he seemed even more capable in person than he does on the screen."

"Well, he's a Special Forces guy, I'd hope so."

"True." She couldn't imagine doing what he did. It was hard enough to make herself go to town and walk around with her limp there. Worse to let anyone see the scars on her back, or the ones around her neck where she'd had to be trached. Dalton? He just let it all hang out, the man genuinely had no fucks to give. "Anyway, when he made the offer and talked to the folks at Brighter Days and Hank's people, they all agreed it was my idea—I should run it."

Why the hell was she beating around the bush about getting to her actual idea? Because she was nervous about it. Nervous about opening up the wounds of her very recent past.

And it's time to get over that. He's here to help and maybe he'll be even more invested if he understands the goal.

"The plan, for what it's worth, is to help female veterans who are homeless to begin with. There's a lot of them who are living out of their cars, some of them with children and some not. They don't always get counted because they aren't on the actual streets. Particularly the ones with kids. They served their country and they come back—sometimes messed up —and they can't hold a job or the job they had isn't there anymore. Bills stacks up..." It was a nauseating cycle.

"I get it. Shit happens. They're veterans, our sisters. So how are we helping them?"

Just like that, Oddjob aligned himself. He was on her team. The sense of dread plaguing her since the accident with the jeep unraveled. "We?" Careful to keep her weight on her left leg, she pivoted to face him.

He met her gaze with a kind of frankness hard to manufacture. The man was like a hero carved right out of the pages of a book. "Hell yeah, we. I'm here for you—and you're here for them. So we."

Damn, she wanted to believe him more than anything else. "Are you hiding some kind of major flaw?"

His eyebrows raised. "Probably."

"Wait...probably?" What kind of an answer was that?

Oddjob's grin spread as he shrugged. "We're all screwed up in our own ways. What you consider a flaw, I might find a feature and vice versa. If you're asking me if I'm perfect? Well, I'll thank you for the compliment and promise to do my best not to let you down. But I'm just a man talking to a beautiful woman about a dream to help veterans. Nothing more. Nothing less."

It took every ounce of discipline she possessed not to say *bullshit*. There was nothing *just* about the man in front of her at all. After considering him a moment longer, she resumed walking and he fell right back into step with her. He'd even shortened his pace to match her much slower one without comment or overplaying it.

Oddjob was definitely living up to his name in all the right ways.

"Anyway," she said, shuttling some of her suspicions to the backburner. Hank vouched for this guy. Hank Patterson, retired Navy SEAL and head of the Brotherhood Protectors earned his reputation for straight shooting in the field and in life. If Hank trusted him, then she would get past her own misgivings. Hope was such a hard pill to swallow.

Faith even worse.

"Anyway," she repeated. "Celebrate will celebrate those veterans by not only giving them a place to get on their feet, but providing access to skills training, medical assistance if needed, and a launching pad to get back on their feet. Montana is a hell of a long way from the bigger cities, but it's also a good place to wipe the slate and start over. For those women with kids, it also gives them a safe place for their kids to readjust and socialize. It's—it's got the potential to be a lot of things and a lot of that is just in my head at the moment."

"Sounds good. You're not ready to open fully, yet?" Less a question than a little digging, but she let that go.

"Six more weeks until our first residents arrive. Two of them are still in heavy therapy at Brighter Days, and one is finishing a rehab program in Texas. She needed to get clean and complete some physical therapy." The number of veteran programs across the country who'd reached out had been overwhelming. "Most of us don't want to ask for help in the first place."

Aligning herself with the residents who would be coming here looking for a fresh start was the first step. She'd walked in their shoes—limped in them so to speak. She'd lived out of a car, and let her pride, and ego prevent her from asking for help from anyone and it had cost her almost everything.

Almost.

"What happens if a person can't get on their feet?" It was a fair question, and she couldn't fault him for asking it.

"We've got plans, and ideas. Not everyone will be a good fit for Celebrate, there are a few other organizations out there doing similar things." Like the one in DC that helped her take the first steps toward independence. "We tackle this one step at a time and the step we're on now is getting this property ready and making sure it's secure. The last thing these women need is to struggle against sabotage and potential physical harm when they are already at the end of their ropes."

"Then we'll make damn sure we're ready for them." Confidence coated every syllable and buoyed her, another reminder that like the women she wanted to help—she wasn't alone.

She needed to remember that. Angling their path through the trees, they'd just arrived at the clearing for the first cabin, a place she might transform for herself once the house was fully done she turned the conversation to him. "What about you, Oddjob? What brought you up to Montana?

They'd made it two more steps when the heat of the explosion ignited and flung her backwards.

CHAPTER 2

No warning could have prepared him for the force of the blast throwing them backward, but Oddjob didn't hesitate. He twisted, pulling Shayna to him and rolling with the blast so he hit the ground first and then tumbled them over so he could cover her. The heat billowed over them, a wash of hot air, and ash. Chunks of wood and splintered boards began to rain down.

Keeping Shayna covered a moment longer, Oddjob checked the angle of the fire and knocked one of the burning boards away. Satisfied the worst of the damage had been done, he rose to his feet. Catching her left arm, he tugged her with him careful not to jerk her. It was bad enough he'd all but thrown her to the ground.

"Are you all right?" He asked in the same breath she turned the question on him. Her expression tightened as she looked past him to the destroyed cabin.

"I'm fine…but the fire."

Trusting her at her word, he pulled the phone from his pocket even as he stamped out some of the flames smoldering around the board he'd knocked away from them. Hank "Montana" Patterson answered the first ring. "We've got a fire here, detonation at a cabin less than a klick northeast of the main house. Cabin is a loss, but we're gonna need fire suppression." Surrounded by trees and verdant green grass, a fire didn't need much to get out of control up here.

"We're on our way." Hank didn't waste time asking questions he could discover the answers for once he arrived.

In the distance, the whinnying of the horses carried. The tension in Shayna's expression gave way to worry. A trickle of blood dripped down from her nose and he frowned.

"Bring a medic with you," he ordered Hank, then hung up. The SEAL had been a damn good man in the field and an even better one here. The Brotherhood Protectors had earned a hell of a reputation via word of mouth and chatter among other veterans said they were the men to go to if you needed a job, a helping hand, or just a break from the rest of the world.

Oddjob had needed all of the above and something much more important. "You're hurt." He tried not to let the words sound like an accusation. Shayna Morgan was more than capable of taking care of herself. He didn't intend to usurp any of the agency she'd reclaimed over the last year—it had pissed him off more than he cared to admit when he'd learned some of her story. The portion Hank shared, which was only that—a portion.

"It's a bloody nose, I'll survive." She was already limping away from him and heading to stamp out another smoldering fire. "We need to drag some hoses from the barn." The pronounced limp had her favoring her right side, and her right hand had curled, the fingers locking. He doubted she was even aware of how she curled the hand inward, toward herself or that she'd tucked her arm to her chest.

Fuck. Had he hurt her when he took her down?

"I'll get the hoses. Stay back from that fire." He was already running for the barn. He could cover the distance swiftly, and they'd come at the cabin via a roundabout, long walk. The gentle pace had eased her stiffness with every step, but the way she'd been hobbling as he left only encouraged him to go faster. At the barn, he checked the horses. They were agitated but all in their paddocks. None of the debris made it this far so he hauled hoses from a rack—three of them. If he linked them together, they would have plenty of reach.

Next he used the ATV to haul the hose back. The accelerated pace would get him back faster, but terrible on his nerves. He couldn't have been gone more than a few minutes, but awareness of Shayna's isolation around the burning remains of the cabin and the fact it exploded in the first place wore at his nerves.

He shouldn't have worried, no sooner did he make

the clearing than she was there and taking the hose and stretching it to a pump that had miraculously survived the blast. He let her hook it up and as soon as the water was on, he was soaking the ground around the cabin, then working his way in toward the remains.

It was still smoking when Hank and the guys got there. They'd brought a water truck with them, and they had it hooked up and were soaking down trees as well as the smoldering ruins. The cabin was gone, anything inside it had been consumed in the blaze. The guys ranged out to check the woods for anything that might have escaped the soaking. Bear took over from Oddjob, using the hose to continue soaking while Oddjob turned his attention to Shayna.

The former Marine glared at the debris as if she could force it to tell her what happened. Given enough time, he bet she could. The blood no longer trickled from her nose, but she also still had her right hand pressed to her chest. Every instinct he possessed screamed at him to take care of her, and get her the hell out of this fire zone. Those same instincts wanted to find the son of a bitch doing this and put them six feet under.

She was trying to rebuild her life in this place, and some asshole was trying to wreak havoc with what she was attempting to build. Fuck. That.

Checking his base instincts, he paused next to her. "Would you like to head back to the house?"

"I want to know who the hell is doing this."

"Copy that. But until the fire is out and they get

the sheriff to bring some arson guys in, we're going to have to wait." Hank likely had some ordinance guys who could look, too. Not wanting to pile on, he added, "I want to do a sweep of the house. You can use the barn apartment to rest if you need it."

Frost skimmed the surface of her gaze when she looked at him and her shoulders pressed back. Dammit, he'd stepped into that one with both feet. "I'm perfectly capable of doing a sweep. Don't try to *handle* me."

"The last thing I plan to do is handle you. You don't need anyone to do that—but at the moment I'm looking to handle my concerns." As much as he'd like to put her behind several armed men in a secure location, he'd take what he could get. "The barn needs to be gone over—and all the other cabins on the property." He'd done a sweep, just like he'd told her, and there were three cabins in addition to the main house and barn. Most of the cabins were in rustic condition, barely featuring running water. They would all have to be modernized.

"You two all right?" Hank directed the question at both of them, but his attention focused on Shayna.

"We're fine," Oddjob answered for both of them. "Soon as she's done here, we'll do a full sweep of the house."

"Good plan. Kujo, Six, and Duke are doing a sweep of the whole ranch. We're looking for how whomever got in—not sure what we'll find. Lots of land to cover." Which just meant they had to be patient. The size of the job never mattered. They were well-trained in how to get it done.

"Need to get a chemical analysis of whatever they used in there." Oddjob sliced a look at Shayna. She hadn't said anything, her gaze fixed on the devastated remains of the cabin. He knew that thousand yard stare, he'd seen it in a number of the guys overseas and at home. It didn't always mean PTSD, but considering what she'd gone through recently—he didn't want to take chances. "Keep me in the loop, we're going to check the house now."

Hank frowned, but he didn't dispute the decision. Montana knew why he was there, and that protecting Shayna was more than just a job. He'd stipulated only one hard and fast rule—if Oddjob couldn't be objective, then he'd be replaced.

Period.

The Brotherhood Protectors liked Shayna Morgan. More than that, she'd survived enough hardship and even then—they weren't sharing all of her story. So whatever ties she had to the group, he could learn on his own. His ties were personal and he wouldn't risk her to anyone else's protection. Not when he owed her his continued existence.

"You ready?" He waited a beat, and her slow blink before she glanced at them confirmed his earlier opinion. She hadn't been with them.

"Thanks for the help, Hank. I'm sorry I have to keep leaning on you."

Patterson squinted at her, then grinned. "Don't be

silly, Marine. We're used to carrying you Marines around."

Her indelicate snort and rolled eyes coupled with a flush of color to her cheeks settled Oddjob down. "Right. Let us know what did that? We're going to have to check the other cabins."

"Already on it. Go check the house. Go over any vehicles before you use them." He gave a pointed look to the ATV.

Oddjob ignored the jab. He'd ridden it more in the interest of getting back to Shayna quickly without considering any problems the vehicle might have. As a point of discipline, he went over the off road vehicle looking for any devices. He'd cleared his share of roadside devices and car bombs. Still, even knowing what to look for—if they'd been moving at a faster pace earlier they would have suffered more than the concussive force of the cabin explosion.

That more than anything else pissed him off.

"I can ride, but I'm not sure I'm up to driving it." Shayna said quietly when she joined him.

"I got this," he assured her. He climbed on and waited for her to settle on the seat behind him. She only gripped him with her left hand and it took her a moment to get her right foot in the proper position. No matter how long it took, he would wait. "Say when."

"I'm good." A catch turned her voice husky. Despite her declaration, he accelerated slowly and let her acclimate to the roughness of the ground and the speed. He took the ATV past the barn. The driveway was gravel, not great for picking up tracks. Angling from the barn he headed up to the house. He wouldn't sleep until he'd gone over every inch of the buildings and they got the results of the explosive tests.

At the house, he waited for her to dismount before he slid off. "How much grief are you going to give me if I ask you to wait here while I do a sweep of the house?"

"Not as much as I will if you go in and get killed if it blows." Was that a hint of a smile? "Besides, two sets of eyes will be better than one and I'd have trouble with the stairs. So you start there and I'll start downstairs. Not that we really know what the hell we're looking for."

Eyeing the house for a moment, he considered the obstacles. "How stuffed is the interior?"

"It's not—we just got the downstairs liveable, and the rooms upstairs are mostly empty."

"Then we check the obvious spots. Electrical. Water heater. Look for what doesn't belong."

"Sound plan." Then she took point, heading up the short three steps to the wide verandah decorating the front of the house. Her steps were halting, and slow. She was hurting more than she'd confessed.

Torn between sending her to sit her ass down and rest and trusting her to handle herself, he stalked behind her. Inside, the house was as large as it looked from the exterior. The front doors opened into a huge, empty foyer with three rooms visibly open to it —a big sitting room and beyond it an oversized kitchen, another room that looked like a second sitting room, and an office straight ahead. A hallway cut towards the back—likely another access for the kitchen and maybe some secondary rooms.

He cut right and up the winding staircase to the second floor. "Is there a basement?"

"Yes."

"I'll check it as soon as I'm done up here." He didn't wait for her response, but cleared the second floor in record time. She hadn't been kidding—the wood floor was bare, and scuffed in places. It needed a good polishing. The bedrooms were bare of any furniture, though there were some paint cans, and tools—including a couple of new frames for windows leaning against the wall in some of them. The bathrooms were bare, the plumbing new, but still requiring the wipe down following an install.

He located an attic door and checked there, checked the plumbing, and then eyed the wall switches.

If he wanted to take down a house, he might set a fuse to the wiring—flip a switch and let it set off a fire within the walls.

Nothing was turned on upstairs and she clearly wasn't sleeping up here. Abandoning the second floor, he hurried down and found her in the kitchen, staring at the stove. "Is it hot?"

"No..." She didn't look away to answer him. "But if I were going to create an incendiary in a house, I'd find a way to tie it into the gas—maybe a slow leak, then ignite it. Hard to escape and fast burning."

He didn't smell gas. "I'd use the electrical system.

Wire it into one of the wall switches, use the flick of the power to set off a fuse, and start it running through the walls…place like this once the walls go— the fire would spread rapidly."

She cut her gaze toward him, and lifted her brows. Lines of tension radiated from the corners of her eyes as she frowned. "Or a combo platter…loosen the gas somewhere, start the slow leak, set off the wall switch and…"

"Boom." Oddjob held Shayna's gaze for a long moment.

"I need my meds, my bedroom is this way." She was already heading there. "We need to call…"

"…someone to do an indepth sweep. Where's the gas valve?" He wanted it turned off. Then they'd go over the barn.

"In the basement, but there's an emergency valve outside."

He followed the trail of her voice and hesitated at the door. The bedroom was on the first floor, tucked behind the office with its bare wooden walls and a desk with a pile of reading material and a laptop. Shayna grabbed a Ziploc bag full of prescription bottles and tossed it into a duffel bag, even at her shuffling and halting step, she kept moving.

"Can you get my laptop from the office, and anything else on the desk?"

"On it."

Five minutes later, they stood outside with a back-pack and a duffel bag, staring at the house. He'd shut off the gas valve and though he'd maintained his focus, he couldn't stop the internal seething. The whole point of taking the job was to protect her, and less than 24 hours on site and he'd already exposed her to one explosion and had her evacuate her house.

"Could be worse," Shayna said, a faint smile curving her lips. "We could be less trained to identify all the ways this could go bad."

A chuckle worked its way through him and he shook his head. "Not sure I'd call that a plus, but I hear you."

She swayed a step as she turned toward the barn. "I'm not sure I want to ride the ATV again." Her right leg wasn't quite keeping up with the left and if he hadn't been watching her, he might have missed the way her gaze dipped to her feet before she straightened her stance.

"Then we walk. I've been through the whole barn this morning." And it had only been unattended for a few minutes. Whoever was harassing her wasn't some prankster. A prankster wouldn't blow up a building. "You can use the apartment and get off your feet if you need it." The last part he tacked on with a wince. He wanted her off her feet, but he didn't get a say—at least not yet.

"That sounds great, but the picnic table will do." Resignation discolored her voice.

"It's hardly comfortable..." It took a moment, but her halting pace struck him. She was moving even slower now than earlier. The limp was far more pronounced, and every step included a harsher exhale from her. "I can carry you up the stairs, Shayna.

Wouldn't be the first time I had to carry a leatherneck after a battle."

She snorted, then released a weak chuckle. The earlier breeze gained some strength, and she reached up to push the dark hair away from her neck revealing a network of scars. Rather than stare, he jerked his attention back to the area around them. The sheriff's SUV currently made its way down the drive.

"Let's talk to him first, then if I'm not feeling up to it, I'll take you up on the offer."

The lack of argument didn't reassure him. If anything, it worried him even more. A woman like Shayna didn't ask for help easily—not even one trained by the military to rely on the guy in front of you and the guy behind. Her being a woman had far less to do with it than her being injured enough she was willing to rely on the assist.

Fine, he'd make sure they had a *quick* conversation with the sheriff.

THE CONVERSATION TOOK FAR LONGER than he cared for, made worse when Hank and Bear joined them. Twice the sheriff consulted Oddjob about something to do with Celebrate—he rather liked the upbeat name for her project—and Oddjob redirected him the first time, then set him straight on the second. Shayna spent most of the conversation on her feet. Hank took the sheriff back to look at the destruction, and Shayna thankfully decided to skip the return visit.

Waiting only long enough for the others to be out of sight, Oddjob raised his eyebrows at her.

"Yes," she managed, and he didn't need any other encouragement. Lifting her carefully, he carried her up the stairs. Despite her trim, athletic build, he carried her up the stairs swiftly. In his arms, she couldn't hide the fact she trembled or downplay the fact that her right hand was almost entirely cramped in a claw formation.

Setting her on the sofa, he deposited her bags on the coffee table. "What do you need?"

"Water," she said with a grimace. "And my pills."

He dug out the Ziploc bag he'd seen earlier, then diverted to the kitchen. A truck pulled in to the drive as he filled a glass with water. It avoided the barn and went straight for the house. Eyes narrowed, he kept watch until he saw Swede exiting the truck and another man stepping out of the passenger side. Oddjob couldn't remember his name, but he and his wife had been visiting with Hank and Sadie when Oddjob had stopped by there a couple of days before.

They had equipment with them—probably a search and scan of the house. Trusting them to do their job, he returned to his companion. Eyes closed, she leaned her head back. The pill bottles were lined up on the coffee table and she cupped several in the palm of her hand.

"Is it bad enough I should get a medic to look at you?" He'd told Hank to bring one, but she hadn't been interested earlier.

"No, it's not that bad—I'm just that weak." She sat

forward and accepted the water glass, then took the pills two at a time and washed them down with a drink.

"Pain is just weakness leaving the body—which makes you the least weak person I know." Her pallor on the other hand served as a stark reminder that she wasn't in good shape.

"Fair point," she said, cracking another wan smile. "I do okay most days—but as evidenced by the cabin, I'm not up for full on field work."

"Well, we'll let it slide. Mission ops didn't include possible explosions in the briefing." He parked himself on the sofa next to her rather than hover. "Hungry?"

"No," she said, draining the glass of water and he took it before she had to lean forward to set it on the table. "I should eat, but I am not remotely hungry."

"MRE? Ramen? Peanut butter and jelly sandwich?" Those were the first three things that came to mind and they were all in his pantry.

"MRE?" Suddenly those dark eyes were focused on him.

"Don't judge. I actually like the damn things. So I pick up a few when I get a chance. They also serve in a pinch when I need to eat and don't feel like fast food or cooking."

"Cause fast food and cooking are the only two options." The humor brought a touch of color back to her cheeks.

"Possibly." He studied the scars he could see. "Are you judging me?"

"Yes," she said with a nod. "I absolutely am. MREs. Blegh."

"Well, I'll have to live with the insult…except I did offer to fix something for you personally." Teasing her was fun, and Oddjob liked the way life seemed to return to her expression. Maybe he should insist on the doctor anyway. Playing it her way was respectful, but the force of the detonation had hit them and he had taken her down in an effort to absorb most of it himself.

Had he hurt her more than if he hadn't?

"True—and I'm sure it would be a gourmet PB&J."

The bark of laughter escaped him and he grinned. "Damn straight, Marine."

Her smile vanished, and she relaxed back against the sofa—or at least she mimicked relaxing. The way she held her right hand suggested it was still hurting, but she'd already begun to massage the palm with her left hand, using her good hand to loosen the fingers on the bad. What the fuck had happened to her?

He had pieces, but not the whole story.

"Can you just call me, Shayna?" The question surprised him

"Sure—don't like being called a Devil Dog? Leatherneck? Marine?"

She grimaced as she straightened her thumb. "It's not a matter of like or dislike. Once a Marine, always one—but…it's like a reminder of another life. One I won't ever get back. I need to learn how to just be Shayna now and to be okay with it."

Humbled, he nodded. "I get that." Well, he did and

he didn't. "Sorta. But I don't have to understand it to respect the request. So—you're Shayna."

"And you're Oddjob." She chuckled, it was a low, husky sound that echoed with pain. Fuck, he hated that she was hurting like this. "I hate to say it, but the name does suit you."

"Aye, better than Fergus." He butchered a Scottish accent just for her. "But me mum ken the folk and wanted to name me after me grandpappy who came over to this beautiful country after the war."

"Good God never do that in public. You might alienate a whole culture."

More warmth filled those cheeks, and a hint of the spark returned to the dullness of her eyes. Satisfied, he plowed forward.

"Ah, lassie, I ken what you mean, but I'm Fergus and I'll always be Fergus..."

"And Fergus is an oddball."

"Oddjob," he corrected, then claimed her glass as he stood. "Oddball was the dog."

More laughter wheezed out of her, and she pressed her good hand to her mouth as she said, "Ow," between the chuckles. He was in the kitchen refilling her glass when she said, "Did you really have a dog named Oddball?"

"Actually?" He twisted and met her gaze.

"Yeah?"

He shrugged, then grinned. "Nope."

More laughter and some of the tension fisting in his chest eased.

"Can I ask how you got the nickname?" The

wheeze in her voice tapered off and she sat a little straighter and even the hunch in her shoulders vanished. Whatever the hell she'd taken had worked. Now he itched to take a look at the pill bottles, get an idea for what she was treating.

"I could…but then I might have to kill you."

The absolute derision in her snort only increased his smile.

"It *could* be classified."

"Right, and you could have a dog named Oddball." No rancor, only more amusement. Good. "I'm starting to recognize where the Odd in your name came from."

He retrieved the peanut butter from the cabinet, and the jelly from the fridge. He put together a couple of sandwiches while he spoke. "You'd be surprised how odd most of us are."

"No," she declared. "No I wouldn't. You're Navy—most of you sailor boys are pretty odd."

"Boy?" He gave her a long hard stare, and she returned his gaze with an unrepentant grin.

"Men go into the Marines."

It was his turn to laugh. "Yeah, my ass rides in Navy equipment."

They were both laughing by the time he carried the sandwiches over. She took hers with a small smile, and a thank you. He saved eating his until he saw how fast she devoured hers. Call him a chauvinist but in his world, the lady got first dibs—Marine or not.

"Anyway," she said after washing down a bite with

a drink of water. "You were telling me about your name."

"I was, wasn't I?" The banter helped improve her mood and her focus. He could do it all day if she needed it. "Sadly, it's not some exciting story. I was in the Air Force—right out of high school. Even got my wings, but it wasn't enough. So requested and got a lateral transfer to the Navy."

She was eating slowly, taking her time in chewing each bite. Her eyes were half-open as she studied him. The last of the tension in her expression eased. Stealing a glance at the bottles he could read, he committed the names of her medications to memory

"I didn't think it would be a big deal, basic is basic —but I landed in a SERE class, and I excelled. Then I started pushing it and one of my instructors said I should consider SEAL training. So I applied...washed out the first time."

She winced. "Ouch."

"Definitely an ouch, I got injured. Failure teaches. I learned. Review board rolled me back, then let me repeat when the injury healed. Second time was the charm."

"Did you get the name because you had to go twice?" Good, she might be a little foggy from the meds, but she still managed to follow his tale.

"Nah, I got it because I was a bird who could swim." The fact they stuck him with a lot of oddjobs in the beginning didn't hurt. "Once I had the name...it fit."

"So you were an Airman, then a sailor, then a

SEAL and now you're a bodyguard. I guess you do get the oddjobs." The fact she vocalized his internal thought pleased him. The woman understood him. A part of him worried he'd manufactured a connection to her and yet, sitting here, even after the destruction at the cabin and her obvious pain, it seemed even clearer.

"I like the oddjobs. This job fits me, too. Kind of like you helping other veterans. It suits you."

"I hope so." She'd eaten most of her sandwich. "Can I tell you a secret?"

"I'll take it to my grave." When he promised something, he never took it back.

"I don't think it's national security secret." The chastisement just made him grin, and he motioned for her to continue. Shifting her position on the sofa, she flexed her right hand. It was opening and closing, though two of the fingers still seemed a little stiffer than the others. "I worry that I'm never going to be well enough for any of it. I have good days and I have bad—and sometimes the bad days really suck."

"Bad days do suck. But you're not a quitter." Nothing about her said give up or run away.

"Shows what you know." She finished the last bite of her sandwich, then met his gaze head on. "I quit once."

"Yeah? Then what are you doing here?"

"Because my uncle wouldn't quit me." There was something more to that story, but he didn't have to ask. "He was in DC, went to see the memorials and do a veteran escort thing. He wanted to see me, and found out I was sleeping in my car, and I couldn't afford my meds, and I couldn't hold down a job. I think if I'd had a gun, I'd have checked out entirely."

Oddjob's blood ran cold.

"I wasn't ready to give up," she said, her gaze taking on that thousand yard stare. "Not really. A part of me kept finding excuses. But my uncle...he pulled me back here, and brought me to Brighter Days. I lived there for the last year, putting my life back together."

"Thank fuck for him, then."

"Oorah."

In that moment, he committed to a second mission. Somewhere along the way, Shayna left herself behind. She was fighting to get back to that woman—the woman who'd saved his life in a desert. A woman who'd given him a reason to live. A woman he'd crossed a continent to find and thank.

It was about damn time he returned the favor.

CHAPTER 3

THREE DAYS after the explosion and they were no closer to the source of the incidents than she'd been when Hank offered Oddjob to help with security. They'd cleared the house, the barn, and all the other structures on the property. Worse, after they went through the debris at the cabin, they'd found no evidence of incendiary devices or a rational explanation for why it exploded. Shayna leaned against the fence railing, watching the horses as they lazed about. She'd turned them out after morning feed, and mentally went down the checklist of things she needed to do.

"Morning boss," Oddjob's voice tingled over her as he came to lean against the fence next to her. He held out a travel mug of coffee. The routine had grown familiar after just a few days. Thankfully, someone had gone back for the mugs they'd lost or maybe he'd had more replacements up there.

"Thank you," she said by way of greeting and cradled the mug. At least the flare she'd endured after the explosion had subsided. Deep stretches each day had freed up some of the tension along her spine and relaxed her arm. Yeah, the new normal was going to take a long time. "How are you doing?"

"Well as could be expected considering age and circumstance." The man didn't have a serious bone in his body. Or at least he managed to play it as if he didn't. Strange, yet adorable in the same breath. "You?"

"Nervous," she admitted. The man could get her to confess to things she didn't even like admitting to herself. Taking a drink of coffee, she tried to contain the follow-up already bubbling to escape.

The weight of his gaze settled on her, and she could almost see his frown from the periphery of her vision but she forced herself to focus on the horses. They were calm, their tails swishing as they ambled along, nibbling at the grass. Of all of them, they seemed the least distressed by the latest events.

So maybe she should take a page from their book. Though she wasn't entirely certain how possible that would be.

"Talk to me, Shayna." Somewhere in that man there had to be a flaw, not that she'd discovered one yet. The need to trust him, coupled with the ease of relying on him seemed like a mistake waiting to happen. Just because she couldn't see the trap, didn't mean it wasn't there. Look at the cabin.

"It's stupid," she said finally, dismissing the unsettled feeling in her gut and taking another swallow of coffee. "We should be getting a delivery today, and I have more paperwork to review. The attorneys sent it over and I'm sure it's fine, but I would rather read it all before I sign it."

"All right," he said, seemingly accepting her response. Then he shifted his position and leaned sideways against the fence. "Are you nervous about the paperwork?"

"What?" Caught, she glanced at him. He'd clipped his beard, neatened the scruffiness and she found herself missing the way it had looked before. "No, it's more about the non profit status, and my appointment to run the facility. I'll draw a small stipend, but I still have to have the ability to sign off on everything. Like I said, I'm sure the paperwork is fine. I reviewed most of the conditions with the attorneys a couple of weeks ago. We're going to be a satellite of Brighter Days Ranch for a time, but the goal is to stand on our own."

"All right, so then the delivery? What's bothering you about it?" He took a long drink of his coffee, but his gaze never moved away from hers.

"Nothing—forget I mentioned it." Giving into the anxiety let it win.

"'Fraid I can't do that. You've been cool as a cucumber since you insisted on sleeping on the sofa." He'd been very clear in his dislike of that choice and his inability to dissuade her when she'd stayed at the barn the night after the explosion. "You said you're nervous, which is not something you'd say lightly.

41

Talk to me. The only thing worse than a bad plan is having no plan at all."

Once they'd gotten the all clear on the house, she'd resumed sleeping there—and if he thought she hadn't noticed his crashing in her living room, he was mistaken.

He came in after she went to 'bed' and left before she 'rose,' but she hadn't slept a straight night through in years. Take the man out of the Navy, but they couldn't take the Navy out of the man—or maybe it was the Air Force and the SEALs too. Either way, he seemed determined to have her back and since he wasn't intrusive about it, she avoided the argument.

And it makes me feel better knowing he's out there. Another sign of weakness that hadn't left the body. She should be able to look after herself, but considering her collapse and backslide, maybe she would never have that privilege again.

Worse, maybe… "We've got a big fat lot of nothing. The jeep's brakes were tampered with, but nothing obvious—they just failed. If it had been the piece of shit I drove around in DC and lived out of, maybe. The jeep though? That was my uncle's and he took damn good care of it." She hadn't told him about the accidents yet, but she'd bet even odds he knew. The Brotherhood Protectors involved themselves damn quick after the first few incidents.

Oddjob didn't say anything. Patience rolled off him, the same kind of calm which wreathed the horses. Maybe that was the source of her discontent. He fit right in on a ranch. The horses, obviously, belonged. So what the hell was Shayna doing there? What did she really hope to accomplish starting this effort here? The veterans she needed to help were in cities...

"The cabin explosion...the jeep. The fact I don't feel like I belong here. It's all making me a little nervous I guess. I'm second guessing the plan. Second guessing myself."

"Then run the plan down with me." He shifted his position and leaned his back against the fence rail.

"Why are you so damn upbeat?"

"Because I'm alive." If she'd placed a bet, this response was not one she would have gambled on. In fact, it wouldn't have even made the top ten. He skimmed his gaze across the wide green separating the house and the barn. "Survival is underrated a lot of the time. We mark our missions by accomplishment, and our service contracts by the number of missions we complete. We look at what we achieve, our rank, our duty assignments, and we say look what I did right. If we get hurt...we tend to say look what I did wrong."

"Or if we lose someone." She could follow his logic.

"Exactly. Now we can beat ourselves up about what we failed, or we can learn from the failure and thrive. I've lost guys...and I've carried guys out. I've seen some of the best men I know lose a limb or end up in a wheelchair. Or worse, in the bottom of a bottle with no discernible way to climb out. So I survive and that means I have a duty to every single one of those who didn't make it all the way back to live the best way I know how and to find a way to make the things that need to happen—happen."

"Dude...you never stop." Admiration vied with envy as she stared at him. "I don't think I've ever been that upbeat before and I did my share of tours over-seas...and in hot zones." Even before women were *allowed* on the front lines of combat situations. They'd been there.

The mistake too many made was considering modern battle lines to resemble those which carved the French countryside in World War I or as if the mythical Mason-Dixon line separating north from south was an actual line demarcating where the battles took place. Women both in service and in civilian life were often caught up in the conflicts.

"So what did you do before?" An element of chal-lenge curled his words.

"Got up and went to work. Reported for duty. Did my job." Damn, that sounded sad now that she thought about it. "The way I was raised, you put up or you shut up. We didn't share our problems with the world, and if we had to limp to put one foot in front of the other, you just did it until it got a little easier."

"You were a real champ at Basic, weren't you?" The teasing pulled a smile from her and she laughed.

"Don't get me wrong, it sucked—but it was the same thing. Get up, do it. Hurt like hell, get some sleep and get up and do it again. Eventually, even the most difficult challenges get easier if you repeat them enough." It was how she made it through classes in high school—the ones that didn't come easy. It was how she learned to ride a bike after wobbling and falling constantly on broken training wheels. Ripped them off and skinned her knees, elbows and even her chin—but she learned.

"What if you couldn't do something? What if you physically weren't able?"

"I don't believe in that." Not even now. "Not even when my body is fighting me every step of the way. I just haven't figured out how to make it work. The day I can't…"

"Don't say it." The order sliced through the air like a verbal slap. "You already told me you were close to making a call you couldn't walk back, don't even suggest it now as a joke."

It wasn't a joke, but… "I hear you. It's a challenge to get up every day and not be certain what you will or won't be able to do. Sometimes, I can go all day, and I'm only a little tired. Other days, it's a physical effort to just get out of bed. My goal is to reclaim every ounce of my independence. Part of why Celebrate is so important to me."

"And why it scares the hell out of you at the same time?" Just like that, he zeroed in on the source of her nervousness and she had to pause to think it all the way through.

"Partially true," she said, but her ready agreement wasn't the whole story. "Making this place work, providing a safe space for other veterans to reclaim their independence is about more than me. If I'm not up the task, if I fail them before we've even opened our doors? I'm not the one who really loses, am I? I tried, if I get pushback and have to start over—I can do that." She could, too. How many times in her life had she had to start again and again? How many times did she reach the top of one wall, all bruised and bloody, only to discover there was a taller one on the other side? "If I fail them, then they lose out on a place to help them pick up the pieces."

"Failing yourself is fine, you'll dust off and go again." He summarized. "Failing others isn't acceptable?"

"No. Not ever." If someone was counting on you, then no. She'd rather drill her own teeth than let down someone to whom she'd given her word.

"Shayna, you're a hell of a woman, but that's nuts." The wry sentiment lacked the heat of a real insult. "If you can't overcome the obstacles here, and you start over—are you telling me that nothing you do in the future will help any of these people you want to help?"

"No, of course not."

"And there are no other organizations out there right now, doing what you're attempting? There's literally no one looking to help these veterans?"

Damn him and his logic. "No. In fact those organizations are part of the reason I want to do this in the first place." They'd helped her.

Straightening, he drained the last of his coffee and she realized, belatedly, she'd finished hers sometime during the discussion. "Last question, do you really think you're in the field alone? Or do you trust me?

Hank? Brighter Days? The rest of the Brotherhood Protectors to have your back?"

She didn't want to rely on them, but that didn't mean she couldn't rely them. "I know they do—I know *you* do." Nothing else could be clearer. Refusing to depend on others was an act of selfishness. One she'd already overindulged.

"Then tell me what's making you nervous right now?" Challenge radiated from him, but more than challenge was a sense of assurance. He needed a target, and he needed her to point him in the right direction.

It was almost too difficult to admit he'd already nailed it.

"I'm nervous about pushing forward and endangering the very people I want to help. I'm nervous that if we leave the property to run an errand, someone will sneak out here and hurt the horses or burn down the house—"

The reality struck her and her stomach clenched.

"And?" He pressed, dipping his head to hold her gaze.

"And I'm nervous that you're planning to be the first one through the door and if I can't have your back, I might get you killed." Fuck. The realization burned, but more than anything else, she'd come to value this man and his crazy name and upbeat attitude.

Oddjob tucked a finger beneath her chin and bent his forehead to rest against hers. "First, we're not dealing with inserting into a volatile situation. We're running defense at the moment, easier to watch the walls than it is to burrow under them." The fact he rolled right into strategizing muted the rapidly ramping anxiety. "Secondly, we've got a hell of a lot of backup and I'm betting we could even pull in air support if needed." Then he winked. "Finally…there's no one else I trust more to have my back."

The last statement stunned her, and she frowned. "I don't get it…why?"

"Story for another day," he released her chin and backed away with a wink. "So, when is the delivery due here? What do you need in town? How long do we need to be out? I'll get us back up so someone is here watching the place for us and we'll take my truck."

Damn SEALs always ready to dive into the action.

Looking hot doing it.

Still, she had to grin. "Groceries…I'm sure as hell not eating MREs willingly."

"Aww," he said, clutching a hand to his chest. "That just means more for me."

Damn, she really hoped she was as reliable as he seemed to think. "I'm going up to the house to make a list. Delivery is due in at two, so if we head into Eagle Rock as soon as someone can get here, we can be back before the furniture truck gets out here."

"Furniture. Check. I'm calling in at least two more guys." The last he tossed over his shoulder as he carried their coffee cups up the stairs to his apartment. Instead of heading for the house, she stared after him.

The nagging sensation of familiarity only increased the more time they spent together. Instead of finding a new friend, it was an awful lot like rediscovering an old one.

And on that note, no more meds. You're starting to sound like a cracked fairytale.

Maybe talking about the issues had been the right thing to do. The grin she wore didn't subside all the way to the house.

CHAPTER 4

DESPITE THE PEP talk he'd given Shayna, the next several days began to wear on his nerves. Following the cabin explosion and subsequent fire, no other acts of vandalism were immediately noticeable. He'd made a point of irregular checks of the perimeter, interspersed with the efforts of the rest of the team. They still had their own lives, though, and jobs. The amount of time passing without incident stretched even his credulity. Shayna's nerves, however, were pulling taut. She checked, rechecked, and paced.

She also didn't bother to hide her lack of sleep. He'd been crashing on her sofa each night, and refused to entertain her suggestion of sleeping upstairs in one of the newly furnished rooms. Lack of sleep in the field was something he could handle. But the passage of time put inordinate pressure on his reserves.

Throwing the idea around with Hank and some of

the other members of the protectors led him to the phone call he currently placed. The guys were all on site—walking a tour with Shayna and one of the facilitators from the rehab facility. Shayna wanted to practice her pitch, and the guys were all interested to see the layout. It meant she was in good hands, but it didn't stop him from keeping an eye out from the window.

It wasn't the first time he'd tried to make the call, but it was the first time Jacko answered the damn phone. "Where the hell have you been?"

"I'm busy Oddjob, how are you?" the other man answered, his tone distracted. When it came to intelligence gathering and dissemination, Jacko was the best man for the job. The retired SEAL did a lot of information scraping since he left the teams.

"Concerned. You too busy to help a friend out? Or do you need backup somewhere?" It would suck if Jacko did, because Oddjob liked to be there for his friends. No way could he step out on Shayna, not until they had her pseudo saboteur-slash-stalker handled.

"Just crocheting some doilies." Jacko didn't miss a beat. "So if you have a good hook stitch, I'll count you in. Otherwise…"

It wasn't always easy to tell when the other man joked or was dead serious. "Roger that. I'm on a job in Montana…"

"Hank "Montana" Patterson is your guy. He's got resources and contacts all over the state. Anything else?" The distracted note promised Oddjob didn't have Jacko's full attention, but the man could do more than walk and chew gum at the same time.

"Yeah, I'm already working with them. Do you want the story or just what I need?" Because he didn't sound like he had as much time for the latter much less the former.

"Fuck, hit me. What do you need?" Just like that, Jacko's attention would laser focus to the issue at hand.

"I need some freelance backup—they stay out sight and out of mind unless something goes down. Decent sized spread here, about two hundred acres, but isolated foot print. Currently two human residents and four equine. That's due to change in about four weeks, but we've had acts of sabotage and at least two attempted murders."

The cabin explosion definitely counted as one and there was no other way to look at the tampering with her brakes.

"High heat? Or just looking for a long slow bake?"

"That's the question, I'd prefer a high heat, burn and dump but we may be sitting on this a while. Lots of action—then nothing." Oddjob rubbed the back of his neck. The tension cording the muscles threatened to give him a headache. He'd been walking a lot, but what he needed was a few rounds with a punching bag—if her harassers didn't show up soon he might need to borrow one to burn off some of the frustration.

"Any chance their lack of success scared off the would be attackers?" The best part of working with others for years, they learned to trust his judgment and asked about the situation—not the way he read it.

"No way to be certain, but my gut isn't sitting right with any of this. You don't go to that much trouble, then back off unless you got what you wanted or…"

"…you're planning something bigger." Jacko got him. "Give me a location, and I'll run some deep background. I'm assuming you think they want this person off the land."

"I can't see anything else she has that someone would want to use terror tactics to take."

"Unless they just want her dead." The blasé delivery didn't gentle the sucker punch Oddjob took to the gut. "What's the lovely lady's name?"

"Shayna Morgan." Rage began to burn in his blood, like phosphorus ready to burn it all to ash.

"Dude…wasn't there a Marine named…"

"Yes there was." He cut him off. "Same lady and I *owe* her." More he liked her. She was damn good people. Circling away from that memory, he gave Jacko the address and GPS coordinates for Celebrate.

"Fuck. All right. I'm on this. My hands are kind of full at the moment, I can send a couple of the guys your way—Flint might be up for it, though he won't thank us if we keep him away from Trudi for too long. Dude is so hung up he can't see straight." Always a good thing. "Angel's up there already running a job with Patterson's group so if he's busy, it looks like Cannon and Mickey are available. Brick's on the road or I'd send him back up that way—but he's somewhere in Kentucky or Illinois."

Flint was like a bulldozer, Mickey had a bit more finesse, and Cannon liked to blow shit up. "Whoever can come, just tell Cannon we already had one blown building—we don't want anymore."

"You got it. Soon as I have something I'll get back to you."

"Hey…" Oddjob said before Jacko could hang up. "You sure you're all right?"

"I'm covered man. Just a lot of irons in the fire. Catch you later." Then Jacko was off the phone. Irons in the fire? The man was a genius with a computer and information scraper. His ability to locate a single thread and use it to unravel the whole thing was a gift, and it had made him an excellent sniper and over-watch. Oddjob was more of a breacher, he took the doors with Flint while Cannon handled their ordinance. Time spent on their team had been one of his best experiences on the teams—though they hadn't been his first assignment, they'd been his last one. One by one, they'd all begun to roll out.

The guys had all landed on their feet, except Jacko's last mission had cost him. Still, he'd healed up and it surprised Oddjob that one of the alphabets hadn't snapped him up—then again maybe they had. Either way, he had backup coming in. Scrubbing a hand over his face, he scratched at his beard. What he needed was a hot shower, a shave, and some rack time —not necessarily in that order.

The group had vanished into the house. Shayna was likely showing them the bedrooms, hopefully she didn't overdo it going up and down the stairs. She'd been damn pleased when she showed him the various rooms—each with its own bathroom. The bathrooms were stocked with a laundry basket, three full sets of standard towels, basic toiletries and grooming supplies.

Two of the shops in town had gathered together donated clothing, all gently used, in a variety of sizes, extra coats, and more. A computer room had been set up, and the kitchen full stocked with utensils, pans, and plates. According to Shayna's plans, a garden would be next on her list—a place for growing vegetables. When he recommended a green house, her eyes had lit up and he could practically see the wheels turning.

Everything she'd committed to was the mission she'd undertaken for herself. The only thing she didn't answer was what she was doing for her. They'd all lived for the mission at one point, but if his time in Texas training with Mateo and his wife had taught him anything, it was that life had to be comprised of more than the just the job in front of you.

Opening a text message, he fired off one before he could think on it too long:

Dinner tonight? You and me? Somewhere we have to dress up?

Maybe he should have waited until she was done showing off the progress so far. He added a second message.

Think about it and let me know when you're done.

Dragging himself away from the window, he strode toward the bathroom. The shower and shave first, if that didn't wake him up, he'd grab an hour of racktime. Hank and the others wouldn't leave without letting him know. Fifteen minutes later, he'd just finished shaving when his phone pinged.

The message was short and sweet.

Sure.

Then she added:

I'm buying.

No, no she wasn't. Pressing a hot towel to his cheeks, he stared at himself in the mirror. "She can pay if she wants to pay." Yeah, even saying the words aloud didn't work for him.

My invite. My treat.

Her response wasn't immediately forthcoming, so he dressed in a pair of jeans in and returned to the window overlooking the house. The crew were outside and she was motioning toward the side where they'd discussed putting in the garden or greenhouse. It would take her time to get back to him.

Crossing his arms, he considered the area outside of the barn—and the story she'd told him about Jacob Dalton. This had been his place before it was donated for her project. What if the issues weren't due to her at all? What if they tied back to Dalton? Maybe their saboteur had been after him and when word got out about her, they stopped...

No. No sooner did the thought settle than he discarded it. Eagle Rock wasn't a big town, and even though he'd only been there a short time, people already greeted him by name or at least recognized the fact he was new. The ranch donation would have hit the gossip mill, particularly with the interest Hank and his crew took in her.

Leaving the window, he threw himself down on the sofa. This was why he didn't like doing *investigative* work. Personally, give him a target and let him take the fight to them. Instead, they had to dig in and wait. If it were just him, fine. But the wait was exacting a toll on Shayna.

They'd figure it out. Jacko was digging, the Brotherhood was on it, and he was here. More, Shayna was paying attention and not fighting the routines they were all employing. The whole thing aggravated the hell out of him because she was at the heart of it. The whole point of coming to Montana was to track her down, and see her again. He wanted to spent time with her, thank her and now that he was here?

He wanted to keep her safe more than anything, get to know her and maybe, just maybe, save her dream the way she'd saved him.

Stop. Running like a hamster on a wheel wouldn't solve anything. He needed rest. Rest and then to figure out what the hell was going on before it closed in on her again.

One arm over his eyes, he told his mental clock sixty minutes. Not one minute more.

AN HOUR before he planned to head over to the house, he caught sight of her limping toward the barn. Grabbing his keys, he jogged down the steps to meet her.

The lines of strain on her face worried him more than the fact she hadn't changed clothes. "Hey…"

"Sorry," she said, and her voice thick with fatigue. "Today took a lot more out of me than I expected."

He offered his arm, and tried to ignore the thrill skating through him when she accepted his support. "Let's get you back to the house. I can cook dinner for you."

"I don't want MREs." The weak joke was still funny, and he slid an arm around her waist so she could lean on him more effectively. If she pulled away even an inch, he'd release her.

She didn't. Fuck, she had to be really hurting. Measuring his steps, he slowed his pace. "C'mon, you know you want some basic stew and heavy gravy. It will be a masterpiece."

Shayna didn't disguise her vague gagging noises, then she chuckled. "Beggers can't be choosers. Maybe we can swindle someone into delivering food. I'd offer to cook, but not sure I'm up for it."

That admission alone had to have cost her. "How about we set you up to relax, and you let me be your hands?"

At the steps to her verandah, he let her take the steps at her speed, and only moved up one at a time along with her. "That's a lot to ask when I wanted to buy you dinner."

"As I recall, I'm the one who asked you out." In the distance, the evening birdsong kicked in. Farther away, a familiar rat-a-tat-tat of a woodpecker. Had to be a big one, to sound so loud. It was the hawk's cry climbing over all of it for a moment which captured his attention. A part of him wanted to twist to look for the bird of prey, but he kept his eye on the prize.

He had to admit, Montana was pretty damn gorgeous in the summer. Warm weather, beautiful trees, stunning landscape really—and Shayna, she'd probably make any area awesome.

"You did, but I said I was going to buy you dinner. You're working for me, remember?" At the door now, he opened it to let her in. Her halting gait worried him.

"We can arm wrestle for it later." The minute the words slipped out, he winced. "Fuck…"

She surprised him with another laugh, even as she pulled away to hobble over to a chair. Once she sank into it, relief crept across her face. "Don't apologize, whatever you do. The fact you were helping me in here and popped off with a comment like that—tells me you don't see me as a cripple. That's something."

Pivoting, he faced her and pinned her with a stare. "Understand something right now, Marine. You may want to adjust to your new normal and not be reminded of where you came from—fine. I'm good with that. But I do know where you came from and I know how you got here. I don't see a cripple, I see a veteran. I see someone who is still paying a cost for saving lives and serving their country."

Not answering him immediately, she swiped her tongue over her lower lip. The action drew his attention to the glistening fullness of it before he focused back on the business of laying the respect between them bare and not imagining baring her skin for more pleasurable pursuits. She was so much more than just some body to find relief in, and his body better damn well remember it.

"Duly noted," she said finally. "It's easier for me to talk smack about how I see myself than to try and fake that it doesn't bother me."

Pinching the bridge of his nose, he wrestled his temper back into a box. Yelling at her for talking down to herself was a dick move. "You do what you need to do—I just want it clear how *I* see you."

A small smile tugged at the corners of her mouth. "You realize you're a walking advertisement for not all heroes wear capes, right?"

Oddjob considered the statement, then struck a pose. "I could handle doing Superman. I think I've got the jawline for it."

"You shaved."

The response wasn't what he was going for, and he paused to rub a hand against his chin. "You don't like it?"

"It's fine…you're a little shaggy around the ears though—and I kind of miss the scruffiness."

"I'll see what I can do for you." Not shaving was something he got used to when they were on the go 24/7, and old habits repeated when he had a lot on his mind. "Now, let's dive into dinner." He rubbed his hands together. "Standing by for orders, ma'am."

"Do you really want to make dinner? There's some microwavable meals…"

"I can do a TV dinner with the best of them, or I

can fix you something real. Just tell me what to do. You have my full attention."

Hell, he knew how to follow orders and what was cooking but following instructions?

"All right," she said, leaning forward even as she flexed her right hand. The stiffness was back. "I think there's some hamburger meat that's defrosted. How do you feel about french fries and hamburgers?"

"I'm feeling like washing and cutting potatoes is a little to on the nose reminiscent of KP duty, but I can handle it." He glanced at the kitchen, then at her. "Do you need anything before I get started?"

"I'm good. Took my meds before I came looking."

"Excellent. Want to tell me about your tour? How it went?" He located the potatoes and carried them over to the sink. Then located a skillet.

"Do you really want to hear about it?"

"I want to hear about everything where you're concerned."

Everything.

CHAPTER 5

SHAYNA ENJOYED WATCHING Oddjob prepare and cook far more than she expected. Despite his earlier claims that he didn't know how, he washed, skinned and chopped the potatoes with efficient, brisk motions.

"I think you've been pulling my leg," she told him. She'd lifted the footrest on the chair, engaging in the recliner function.

"Never said I couldn't cook." The glib remark had her smile widening. "Plus, my parents run a restaurant. I can do just about anything with potatoes— including shredding them for the most perfect hash browns you've ever eaten."

Her stomach rumbled. "Now you're teasing me."

"Could be. So c'mon, tell me about the tour." He made short work of the potatoes then got oil heating on the stove.

"It went great, everyone was happy with the progress, and they like the rooms. Swede suggested we add on a gym of some kind. I like that idea, maybe add an indoor pool to go with the greenhouse." The meds were working, she was reaching that humming state where yes, she still hurt but no she didn't care as much. The doctors told her it would take time, and she had to be patient and do her therapy. Avoiding stress had also been mentioned, but unless she was dead stress was a fundamental part of life.

"Huh, that'll take more investment I'm betting." He washed his hands before he got the hamburger meat out and began shaping the patties.

"Definitely more than what we have in the budget. I have some ideas for fundraising though." A side aspect of the project she hadn't considered before diving in. Managing the property would take more than just her willingness to share her experiences with others. "Not a skill I've honed, but I thought I'd start with reaching out to some of the various veteran organizations that have already pledged funds over the next year and describe what I think are the benefits."

"Let me know if I can help—I'm a mean typist." He waggled his hamburger coated fingers at her. "I could be your Guy Friday."

Chuckling, she shook her head. "First, I have to research the costs, and put together projections. Then build a presentation. I'm thinking a video with me gimping around the area I want to transform, then using my own medical records to demonstrate why gardening, swimming, and regular exercise could improve my self-reliance, self-image which would then drive my independence." Stretching her bad arm, she added, "All of which are one hundred percent true."

"You're going to open a vein for this place, aren't you?" Admiration tangling with concern clouded the question.

"If I want it to work...yes." She liked Oddjob more than she cared to admit, or maybe more than she believed possible. The man was just comfortable to be around. He treated her like a person, a capable one and he never overstepped. Never rushed to do something for her unless she asked for help. Did he have any idea how amazing he was? "It's easy to forget that you're a person when your condition is so much a part of your life. It's easy to forget your own strength, and perseverance when it takes every ounce of your willpower to do something like make a meal or take a shower."

There was power in saying it all aloud. Power in owning her frailties and the confusion of emotions which went with them.

"It's harder still when you have to admit you can't do it all, that the skill you spent so much time honing isn't available to you anymore." Like protecting the place she wanted to build. "Before you give me the team lecture, I get it—here." She tapped the side of her head, then lowered her hand to press over her chest. "Here though? Here it gets messed up with being less than who I am."

The sizzling of the burgers he added to a pan

joined the crackling of oil cooking the potatoes. Damn she was starving.

"I get that—mostly." Oddjob admitted. "There's a Marine, retired, I worked with down in Texas. He and his fiancée train therapy horses. He just had a surgery to help correct some of the nerve issues he has and he was able to ride again. It's a work in progress, or so he says."

If a surgery could fix her, she'd do it in a heartbeat. "I'm not there yet. I can ride as long as I go slow. The damage wasn't just from the bullet—though I did take one. It's more because the body armor failed." The sound of bullets slicing through the night air. The hum of them whizzing passed. The curious little thunk they made when they impacted against the armor. The slam driving all the air out of her lungs, and the tumble. Then the godawful cracking noise, and white hot pain shattering the night. She blew out a shaky breath.

Oddjob flipped the burgers, but his gaze locked on hers. "You survived."

Perspiration beaded her forehead and her pulse fluttered faster. "Easier said than done."

"Yeah, but you did it. Every day you get up. Every day you don't give in. Every day you keep building. You survived." Absolute certainty and faith reflected in his gaze.

"Has anyone ever told you that being perfect is intimidating?" Tears gathered in her eyes and she blinked them back.

"You don't intimidate me, lady," he said with a

slow grin, and a wink. "You just challenge me to be better."

Watery laughter escaped her. When he turned to remove the burgers from the pan, she swiped away her tears. A few minutes later, he joined her with two plates piled high with burgers and fried potatoes.

"Thank you," she said before taking her first bite. He'd added cheese, and some mustard for her. His had ketchup and sliced tomatoes—which seemed overkill, but she wasn't going to complain.

"My pleasure." The way he framed the words, they were a caress gliding over her skin.

"So when you're not baby sitting me and cooking amazing meals, what do you do with yourself?"

"Help out at my parents' restaurant in Ohio. I grew up there near Lake Erie. Small town, lots of folks who are tight with each other. There's a few factories there, thought about going home to work but...last time I was there, I didn't fit anymore. Or maybe it just didn't fit me." He paused to take a bite of his burger, and she tucked into the potatoes. Her rumbling stomach gurgled its approval. She shouldn't have skipped meals in her rush to get everything done, hunger and overexertion taxed her limited resources.

"I could have gone home, you know. Called someone when the bills piled up. I was having trouble getting out of bed in the morning and I kept calling out sick from work. The writing was on the wall... then the notices for nonpayment. I stopped answering my phone because of collections." Not her proudest moment. "I told myself I wasn't going to ask for help because I didn't want handouts."

He dabbed a napkin against the corner of his mouth, clearing away a speck of ketchup. What would it be like to lick it clean? The chiseled strength of his jaw captivated her. Despite what she'd said earlier the man was gorgeous with or without his beard. "My dad would have brought a beat down on my ass if I didn't let him help."

Yeah, she couldn't picture any man having that kind of an effect on him.

"Between you and me, my mom is scarier. She's got this look…" He schooled his features and stared at her, the absolute lack of expression even more intimidating than a scowl. "You can't read what she's thinking or feeling, but you know your fate is in her hands."

Shayna snorted. "My uncle can do that—in fact he did. God, waking up that day to him knocking on the car window. I'd rather take Baghdad."

"Right?" Oddjob's grin returned and he shook his head. "Anyway, I went home and it didn't fit. I think I've always been restless. The military answered a lot of that for me, but I spent some time with buddies who were out and then I went down to Texas to train. I like horses. Working with them could be fun."

"But you're still taking protection work?" Working with animals she got. Restlessness she got. But why take a bodyguard job?

"On a case by case basis." Now there was a hedge.

"And my case appealed to you?" She'd already

devoured most of her burger, and he'd made more than one. She could go for seconds. Studying him, she could go for thirds, too.

"You appealed to me." Just like that they weren't talking about his work or history.

"Were you born tattooed with the word super hero or did you just work to achieve it?" Fresh perspiration dotted the back of her neck and it had nothing to do with her past and everything to do with the man sitting across from her.

"I'm just me and besides, the real hero is the one who gets burned but goes back in. Keeps pushing. You were down. You got up. Doesn't matter how, you did it. No one can take a crap for you."

"Oh my God," she laughed, and had to stop eating lest she choke. "You should get that put on a t-shirt."

"Like that, did you?" He winked. "It's the truth, call it salt of the earth wisdom or at least what my grandmother used to say to me. She had to keep the family business going, and raise six kids while her husband was in Korea, and later when he went to Vietnam as an advisor. She didn't take crap from anyone. She used to say life was what we made it to be. We couldn't take a crap for someone, we could just help them dig the hole. We couldn't change the past, but we could help pave the future. She was a tough old bird and even when I got tall enough that I towered over her, I could never top her spirit."

Shayna liked her already. "You miss her."

"Hell yeah." Regret stamped his features. "She passed away when I was on a covert op. I was out of touch for six weeks. I missed her funeral, too. Not that she would have cared."

No, from the sounds of it, she'd probably have been annoyed if he'd dropped any balls to run home. "Doesn't change the fact you hurt over it."

"Pain is life." Another little kernel of wisdom. His plate was empty, and he stood glancing at hers. "Want more?"

"Yeah," she said passing him her plate, but she put the foot down on the recliner and stood.

"I'll get it," he told her, but he didn't wave her off.

"I know, but it's good to stand. Meds are working and there's food in my belly. The pain is much more manageable now." Besides, walking got her out of the damn chair and helped her move. The more she moved, the looser she got and the short walk to the kitchen was hardly running around the block. "Sometimes, it's easy to let the pain be in charge. You can't let it take over. If it hurts, and you press a little and it just hurts more—I back off and regroup. Then I go again."

In the kitchen, he built two more burgers on the plates and split his attention between them and her. "Nana would have liked you. She did her own grocery shopping and lived on her own until the day she died. She had a walker, and couldn't get up and down the stairs. Survived a hip replacement, and kept right on trucking. She said you're only as old as you behave."

Unable to resist the charming way he lit up when he talked about her, Shayna circled the island and leaned against him. "Does that make you five?"

Setting aside the burger, he wrapped an arm around her waist and eyed her. "Babe, I'm definitely not five."

The air seemed to fill with an electric charge. When he dipped his gaze to her mouth, she almost held her breath. The moment elongated and it hit her. He wanted to kiss her but gave her the first move. Rising on her tip toes, she braced a hand against his chest. "Not sure I can stretch that far."

One moment she leaned against him, and the next he set her on the island right next to the food. It brought her head level with his and she didn't have to tilt her neck to far. Gliding her hand over his smooth jaw, she whispered, "I think the shave is growing on me."

"Yeah?" He leaned into her and his breath tickled her lips. The scent of food and man twisted around her, even more enticing than the meal.

"Yeah, but we may have to test the theory." She licked her lips and closed the distance, the lightest of brushes. Fuck, she'd forgotten what it was like to be this close to another human being. To have the heat of their body pressing against hers. Positioned between her legs, she touched her knees to his hips. What started out a gentle whisper of contact turned molten when his mouth claimed hers. He braced his hands on the counter on either side of her, and then his tongue teased along the seam of her lips.

Opening to the kiss, she glided her hand up to the thickness of his dark hair and desire rang through her. The collision of need and want twined together as he deepened the kiss, and then she had her arms around his neck and he locked one hand against her hip. The simple restraint in this powerful man stripped her to the core, and she broke the kiss long enough for a breath.

"Hi," she whispered, meeting his smoldering gaze.

"Hi," he returned, then brushed another gentle kiss to the corner of her mouth. "How are you?"

Laughter and sighing were impossible to do at the same time, and yet she managed. "I'm having a really good time."

"Yeah?" He traced his fingers up her side, then glided them along her neck. A self conscious part of her roused at the contact. The network of scars from various procedures weren't pretty. The rest of her marveled at the tingles—pleasurable this time—cascading over her. It was too much and not enough in the same breath.

"Yeah…I remember when touching hurt." Then she closed the distance again, and relegated the knee jerk fear of contact to the back of her mind. Fear had no place in this moment, not with her and definitely not with Oddjob. Stroking his tongue with hers, she leaned fully into the act, trusting him to keep her braced and safe.

He palmed her cheek, and then the whole world narrowed to the singular contact of his mouth on hers. To the glide of his lips, the tease of his tongue, and the molten heat gliding through her veins.

The world shook. All of it.

Then the sound penetrated the haze, and he lifted

his head breaking the contact, even as she jerked. Pain eddied through the shock.

"I didn't imagine the world shaking did I?"

"In more ways than one." He lifted her off the counter and set her on her feet before striding to the front door. The whinnying of the horses carried in on the breeze and in the distance, black smoke wafted through the sky. "Son of a bitch…"

CHAPTER 6

STINKING of smoke and covered in black soot, Oddjob glared at the smoldering remains of another burnt out building. Fortunately this one wasn't on Celebrate's property but a neighbor's. He and Shayna came over on the ATV, following the smoke. Despite her earlier pain, she refused to leave until they had it all out. It didn't take long for word to spread and more help to show up.

Fires this time of year didn't take long to get out of control. Tempers were burning high, too. The sheriff ordered everyone away from the husk once the fire was out. An arson investigator had also been called in. Check ins with the Brotherhood Protectors and the imminet arrival of Flint and Mickey didn't allay his concerns. Someone, somewhere was doing something.

Accidents. Explosions. Fires. No one had been genuinely hurt—yet. It was the yet he didn't like.

He'd give Mickey and Flint the barn apartment as a base of operations when they arrived the next day. Cannon had been delayed to help Jacko out with something.

Hank and his team wanted to run some leads down, not that they had many. Frustrated with their lack of progress—with his own lack—he took Shayna back to her place. It took him a few minutes, to double check the interior. The fact the security system was on didn't satisfy him until he'd checked every room. The burgers he'd made earlier were cold, and the potatoes were soggy but neither he nor Shayna complained as they ate.

"You should shower," he told her.

"You need one too," she told him, the fatigue in her voice another reminder that she'd already been spent before they spent half their night out fighting a fire, and checking—then rechecking the barn. She wouldn't rest until they'd made sure the horses were okay. "Maybe I should call over to Brighter Days and have them take the horses for a while."

His gut clenched at the hint of defeat sneaking into her voice.

"I wouldn't be able to forgive myself if something happened to them."

"We'll make the call in the morning," he assured her. "I'll keep watch and split my patrol between the barn and here in the morning. So far, everything they've hit has been unoccupied."

"Except my jeep. I was definitely in my jeep."

Oh yes, he remembered that part. Sliding his hand

to her cheek, he ignored the soot and dirt and pressed his lips to hers. A gentle, single kiss of affection and warmth. A reminder she was still with him. "They didn't blow that up." Thank God.

"True." When she wrapped her arms around him for a hug, he held her to himself. The fact she willingly leaned on him soothed the raw places in his soul. The spots eaten away by the acid of his failure to keep her safe. It didn't matter that he hadn't been there when the incident happened, what mattered was she'd been put there in the first place.

He wanted her as far from all of this as possible and he had no damn right to ask her, much less push for it.

"You okay?" She hadn't pulled away, instead, she leaned there as she ate her cold burger. Spreading his fingers against her back, he rubbed slow, gliding circles. Her back had been injured, and he didn't want to add to it. When she sighed under the contact, he added a little more pressure. It calmed him further.

"I'm pissed off," he admitted. "I want to find whoever is behind this and break both their legs." Maybe all their fingers, and toes, too.

"Torture is against the law."

"True," he agreed, undeterred. "But I'm a little old school, eye for an eye and all that."

The dry comment worked, and she chuckled only to have a cough interrupt it. He released her long enough to grab a glass of water for her. The medics checked their throats since they'd been out there battling the blaze. Still if hers was at all like his, it probably hurt.

She took the drink, then glanced at him. "Is it okay if we go back to the me leaning on you?"

"Why don't we sit down and you can even sit in my lap if you want?"

For a moment, she appeared to consider the invitation then said, "We stink and I don't want to get it on the furniture." After finishing the last bite of the second burger, she drained the water. "Showers, then we can do a sleepover in my room."

Every drop of his blood pounded south at the invitation, but he hadn't lead with his dick since he'd been in high school. He wasn't starting now. "You sure?"

"Don't get excited, big boy." She patted his chest. "I said sleepover...and yeah, I'm sure." Sobering, she eased away from him. "We both know you've been sleeping on the sofa. You're worried about me, and I'm worried about you. And...truth be told. I don't want to be alone right now."

Fair enough. "Okay, I'll run upstairs and shower. You shower in your room. Meet at your bed in ten?"

"Give me fifteen...a girl needs time to wash her hair and look pretty."

Cupping her chin, he locked his gaze on hers. "Maybe girls do, but you my sweet, sexy Marine? You always look gorgeous." Then he punctuated the affirmation with a kiss before striding for the stairs. He had a duffel stashed up there with some clean clothes. It only took him five minutes to wash off the dirt and soot. Another two to brush his teeth after he pulled on shorts and a t-shirt. He normally slept naked, these were a concession to sleeping at her place.

Back downstairs, he sent a message to the team on patrol for the night, and made sure the security system was armed. He'd armed it when he came in, but he always double-checked. After another sweep of the house, he checked the cameras they'd installed on the barn. The motion sensor was sensitive, but not too much or the horses would set it off.

However, if something startled the horses the sudden jerks would get its attention. He'd been busy the last few days and Hank's guys had lots of ideas. Mess with one of theirs, and you dealt with all of them—Oddjob included.

Satisfied, he set the dishes in the sink. He'd wash up in the morning, then he made his way to her room at the fifteen minute mark. Though the door was partially open, he knocked once and waited.

"Clear," she called and he pushed the door in. She was already propped up in the bed, pillows piled behind her and two under her left knee, elevating the leg. Like him, she'd slipped into shorts and a t-shirt. Where his were blue and white, she'd gone for solid gray, and the shirt said 'bite me.'

"Is that an invitation?" He couldn't resist asking as he eyed the positioning, she was on the side closest to the door. No, he wasn't a fan. Of course, his side would be closer to the window. Checking his base need to be between her and all access points, he settled on the side she'd left free for him.

"No, just my general comment for life in general. Being pissed off at it helps sometimes."

"Truth," he agreed and stretched out, a sigh escaped him. Damn, he was tired. Tired. Sore. Aggravated. But more, he was turned on just being close to her. Leaning over, he brushed a kiss to her cheek and then drew in a deep breath of her clean, fresh scent. "You smell great."

"Right back atcha."

He stretched out an arm. "Cuddle?"

Surprise flickered through her eyes and she raised her eyebrows. "A kiss and a cuddle?"

"I'm never going to tell you no to more, but you're tired and I don't know what will hurt you or not. So in this, you take point. I'll have your six every step of the way." The honesty robbed him of nothing. The idea of going down on her until she screamed her orgasm had been on his mind more than once.

"You really are perfect," she groused, then eased off the pillows to crawl into his lap. An honest to god shudder seemed to race from his cock to his spine at the warm heat of her resting against him.

"Fuck no, I'm not." He cupped the back of her neck, and placed a hand on her hip to ease her into a more comfortable position. The last thing she needed was his boner shoving her in the ass.

And he really shouldn't have let his thoughts go there.

"I'm a red-blooded male, and you are a sexy as fuck woman. I'm not kidding about letting you drive where this goes, but the idea of stripping off this shirt, sucking your nipples as I let my hands explore every inch of your skin is definitely at the top of my list, but not quite as high as sliding my fingers into you and—"

She didn't let him finish because her mouth closed on his, and her teeth scraped over his lower lip. The boner he sported grew more intense, and weight of her pressing into him set fire to even more demanding thoughts.

Drowning in the kiss, he waged war against his instinct to take over, to tumble her onto her back and drive away any thoughts of hurting ever again.

Gasping for a breath she pulled back. "I don't know what will hurt or not…I haven't had sex since before I deployed on the mission that ended with me in a hospital bed and them pulling fragments from around my spine. I've got scars—my scars have scars and at one point, even air touching me hurt."

Easing his grasp, he frowned. "Don't hurt for me. I can just hold you. Or sit next to you…"

She traced a finger over his lips. "You aren't hurting me. I just don't know how much I can take when I want all of you."

The words pulled a groan out of him and nipped her fingertip. "Then we go slow…test what you can handle, and what you can't."

If she said no, he and his hand would need a date and soon. For now, he waited. When she eased away, he released her. Then she gripped the hem of her shirt and met his gaze.

"Fair warning…this isn't that pretty."

"Shh, don't badmouth my hot as hell Marine." The

possessive slipped out but he wasn't going to shy away from it. He wanted her.

All of her.

Not just to save her, or help her get her life where she wanted it. He wanted the woman he'd gotten to know. The fiery spirit, determined independence, and relentless need to serve. He wanted *her*. Scars and all.

She tugged the shirt off, and his gaze went to the supple curves of her breasts. They weren't large, but they were perfectly crowned by a dusky nipples already pebbled to points. His mouth watered and he extended a hand, slowly cupping one and tracing his thumb over the tense point.

At her swift indraw of breath, he checked her expression. "If anything hurts…*anything*, you tell me."

"Yes sir," she exhaled the words on another shudder of breath as he rolled the nipple between his thumb and forefinger. Fisting his control, he took his time, teasing one breast, then the other. When she closed the distance, he took over the kiss thrusting his tongue against hers in a move to mimic what his body wanted to do to hers.

She twisted, returning to his lap and straddling him. Dropping his hands to her hips, he steadied her and waited until she sank down. The brush of her heat over his groin, even separated by clothing threatened his sanity.

But he was a SEAL, he could handle it.

This wasn't about his needs, but hers. Then she was kissing him again and her breasts pressed against his chest. He slid his hands over her ass, cupping and squeeze. When he teased a finger along the inseam, a delightful dampness greeted him and she shuddered. Then she kissed along his jaw and bit his earlobe, the sting chased away by the lave of her tongue.

"I want you, Oddjob." The words an affirmation, and declaration. "I don't know if I can do slow."

"Tell me what you want," he ordered, as he pressed his finger farther. The lack of panties beneath her shorts let him ease a finger right against her slick channel, he dipped in a knuckle length then out. Swirling the finger over her clit, he reveled in her sudden gasp and grip on his shoulders.

"You," she admitted, shaking. "I want to feel you."

Another press of his finger elicited another wild gasp and he checked her expression. The dilated pupils, the flush to her skin coupled with the short shallow breaths and he stroked her clit until she released a soft cry. Savoring her every reaction, he caught her when her muscles trembled and threatened collapsed. Shifting, he rolled her onto her back and with care, he peeled her shorts away.

"Still with me?" He whispered, pressing a kiss to a puckered scar at her side, the remnants of bullet wound. Just below it was another ripple of ribbed skin, a pink slash against tan skin. A flesh wound, perhaps?

"Yes," she breathed, holding a hand out to him. "All clear for insertion."

That should really not sound as dirty as it did, but he laughed and teased her lips with a brief kiss before he took a long, leisurely trip down her torso. He wanted a taste—needed one. Another pebbled, grated spot on her right thigh. It looked like a burn, perhaps. Or some other wound.

"I told you, not pretty." She'd twisted slightly to gaze at him.

Pressing a kiss to that scar, then traced it with his tongue. "Life isn't always pretty, but I love these… each one is a testament to your continued survival, and that you lived long enough for me to find you."

When she didn't respond immediately, he glanced up to find she'd pushed up on her elbows even though her right arm trembled violently.

"Easy," he said, reaching for a couple of pillows to slide behind her. He didn't want her hurting. He'd been clear on that.

"You—take my breath away."

Grinning slowly, he rubbed a hand along her thigh. "Then I should make sure you can catch it before I give you another kiss."

"You don't have to," she assured him, eyes shining. Then she sucked her lower lip between her teeth as if holding back what else she had to say. Never looking away from her, he pressed her thighs apart then dipped his face to press a carnal kiss against the clit he'd already tormented.

This time when she sighed, it echoed in his soul.

CHAPTER 7

SHAYNA'S new normal hadn't included sex, no matter how attractive the men around her. She hadn't been kidding about how even air hurt her when she first woke up in recovery, nor how badly she hurt in the intervening months. Every sliver of progress she made came at an intense cost of pain. With Oddjob's hands on her, all she experienced was pleasure. When his lips locked on her clit, she forgot to think and just let the pleasure thread through her system.

The orgasm his tongue elicited from her stormed through her system. Even as she trembled from the ride, he was climbing along her body. His mouth closed over hers and she wrapped her arms around him. Somewhere along the way he lost his clothes and she savored running her hands over his muscled chest, and back. Like her, he had his share of scars.

She rode the eddying waves of her orgasm down as he casually began to drive her mad all over again.

When he finally slid a condom on and he eased into her, her bliss shattered on another wild wave. Every thrust grew in with intensity and force as if he measured how much she could take.

A part of her wanted to scream at him to make it rough, but she wasn't sure if she could take that and so she gave him the lead, clinging to him as he filled her over and over. The weight of his body pressing into hers offered more than pleasure. It was security, comfort, desire, and strength all wrapped in one sexy as hell package.

A second orgasm so close to the first left her body buzzing, and the pins and needles rioting through her system only emphasized the wildness unfolding within her. He stiffened against her and she opened her eyes in time to see his expression go taut as he came.

The storm carried them both, and when he finally collapsed, she arced a leg over his hips and press kisses to his head. His body seemed fused to her, and she couldn't believe she touched him everywhere and so intimately and all she felt was good.

"Am I too heavy?" He asked, his breath warm on her ear.

"Don't move," she ordered. "Stay right where you are."

"Yes, ma'am." The ease of agreement offered another boon to her existence.

"I love this," she whispered, stroking her fingers through his hair. "I can feel you, the heat—the pressure…it's glorious."

Her inner walls spasmed as little waves of after pleasure washed through her. He let out a grunt, and then chuckled. "You're so damn hot, woman. I never want to leave."

Forever was a long time, so all she said was, "I'm not kicking you out of bed."

"Thank God." Then he nuzzled her throat, and cradled her. They lingered like that for minutes or maybe it was hours. She lost count, drifting on the lazy haze of warmth surrounding her. When he did move, it was only long enough to dispose of the condom, then he pulled her back to him, and cradled her in the bed. Normally she slept on a half dozen pillows to keep herself and her shoulders propped. This time, he propped her back against his chest and provided all the support she could want.

Hand in hers, he threaded their fingers together. "I have a confession," he told her in the dark.

"If you're married, I don't want to know." Maybe it was selfish, but she couldn't handle that at the moment.

"Fuck no," he said, his tone harsh. "I'm not a cheater. When I commit to someone, I'm all in. You have me right now, and for as long as you'll keep me. Got it?"

She didn't quite cheer, but she squeezed his hand. "Good. Be careful, I might keep you."

A kiss to her temple, his breath teasing her scalp. "That's what I'm hoping—but first, I have to tell you something."

"Well, I already know about your love of MREs, it can't be anything worse than that."

Silence. Then warm masculine laughter flooded the room and his chest shook against her back. The vibration was almost as good as sex, but she'd keep that part to herself. "No more comments from you, ma'am. Not until I'm done."

"Sir, yes, sir."

"Smartass." But he cupped her breast as he spoke, and squeezed her nipple. The sharp pleasure a spear through her sensuous fog. "Beautiful, sexy, hot smartass. And the woman who saved my life."

"What?" She blinked, and wished they weren't spooning in the dark so she could see his face.

"About a decade ago, I was assigned to a medic team—this was a few months before I went to BUD/S." The calmness in his voice twined around her. "We were backup ops, support. Moving through cleared areas, tending to the wounded both military and civilian. I was on guard duty."

He used a thumb to tease a circle against her hand. "Boring, or so I thought at the time. We were far from the action. What was going to happen?"

Lots of things could happen, but she kept quiet.

"Arrogance is the province of the untrained. A small contingent of insurgents came out of nowhere, they opened fire, pinning me and the medic closest to me down. I couldn't get him out and our cover was taking a beating. I had to get my guy out, and I was willing to take the hit for him. Somehow, one of them got behind me and I turned to find myself face to face with a guy who couldn't have been much older than me. He had the drop though, and I had just enough time to say a prayer…when a sniper took him out."

This sounded vaguely familiar.

"One by one, the sniper took most of this group, saving my life and everyone with us." He chuckled. "By the time I got a chance to ask, the only thing I could find out was a Marine attachment close to our location heard the fire and came to help. No one knew who the sniper was—just a jarhead."

Shayna bit her lip. "I remember that day…"

"Yeah," he told her, then kissed the shell of her ear. "So do I. I remember thinking I owed that Marine everything, I owed them to be better at what I did, to be the one who swooped into the middle of the fire-fight to help out people whose names I didn't know."

"How did you find out it was me?" The fact he'd told her at all left her a little in awe.

"A friend of a friend of a friend, pulled the names. It had been classified at the time, and no one listed the Marine in their duty reports—not the specific one acting as sniper."

No, they wouldn't. She wasn't supposed to even be in that location. They'd been running a classified op, and she was the only translator available. "Most of us look the same in our gear. Hard to pick out the girls."

"You saved my life Shayna, you didn't know it was me or who I was or anything. You saved my life and you changed it."

Tears burned in her eyes and all at once she was grateful for the darkness.

"I've waited over a decade to say...*thank you.*"

Sniffing once, she squeezed his hand. "You're welcome."

Then he nuzzled her head and she sank into him. She hadn't thought he could be more perfect.

She was wrong.

THE NEXT FEW days fell into an almost blissful routine if one discounted the fact that they'd had to put out two fires, still didn't know the identity of the saboteur, and existed on edge most days. Oddjob's friends arrived to help alleviate the pressure on the Brotherhood Protectors and split up the patrol work. They moved into the apartment over the barn while Oddjob stayed with her.

Everyday, they went over the property and she continued building plans and estimates for the suggested changes. Every night, she went to sleep in Oddjob's arms. He also seemed to pick up on the cues she was hurting before she did, and he helped her stretch when she needed it, and carried a small container with her pills in case she forgot them.

The latest lead they had was on a potential buyer for ranches in the valley. Paul Dryden had been visiting a number of the ranchers and making offers. Though she hadn't seen him, they had a call into Jacob Dalton to see if he'd received an offer. Dryden wasn't a local and maybe he didn't know about the donation.

"I don't get it," she said, leaning away from the laptop. Numbers sucked, and she embraced the distraction even if it was about the person causing Celebrate issues. "Why would someone interested in real estate set these fires? How would they do it?"

"Don't know, don't really care why. If it is him, then we find him and we stop him." The longer this dragged on, the fiercer Oddjob became. It was a personal affront to nearly all of them that they hadn't figured it out yet. "All I know is whoever it is, doesn't seem to be acting in a predictable pattern. We thought maybe it was a personal ax to grind with you."

"Except the cabin fire next door doesn't link up." She'd thought about it, but to her knowledge she hadn't offended someone enough to come after her so viciously. At least, she didn't think she had.

"Unless they didn't realize where the property line was." The cabin that had gone up was an old hunting cabin just on the other side of the lines between the ranches. No one had used it in years, and it had a well for water, but no electricity. They'd still gotten lucky.

"We can't borrow trouble, we have enough as it is…" She trailed off when his phone rang.

"I gotta take this." He pressed the key to answer it, then lifted it to his ear. "Jacko, tell me you have something." Whatever the man had to say, it was lengthy. Oddjob frowned then said, "Hey I'm putting you on speaker, run that down again."

Then he put the phone on her desk.

"Copper mining. I've been pulling assay reports, but that name you sent me—Paul Dryden, he's all over them. The location you're sitting on is listed as being over one of those copper deposits or whatever. Don't ask me how this shit works, but if I were a betting man—which by the way I'm not—then I'd hazard this is why Dryden is trying to buy up ranches. Has he made an offer on that place?"

"No," Shayna answered. "As far as we know. We're still waiting to hear back from Mr. Dalton. This was his ranch, he donated it to the project."

"We can get into that…here's the thing, depending on how they are doing the mining, they could have come up at those cabins or pumped gas up below them. They could have detonated them and boom, bang, Bob's your uncle, blam." That was a colorful way of describing it. "According to online encyclopedia, copper mining requires a tunnel or open pit. I'm pretty sure you wouldn't miss an open pit, so I'd be looking for a tunnel."

"If you were a betting man." Oddjob's tone was dry, but thoughtful.

"Exactly."

Silence blanketed them.

A copper mine? "Copper is not that rare…would someone really go to that much trouble over one mine?"

"It's a 1.3 billion dollar industry," Jacko replied. "People will kill for a jug of milk. You do the math."

"Hey," Oddjob snapped. "Watch your tone."

"Ma'am," Jacko tacked on as if an afterthought. "No offense intended."

"None taken. Thank you, Jacko."

"You're welcome, see how that works, Oddjob. You ask me for a favor you say thanks. Gotta go. Let me know if I can do more." Then he was off the line and Oddjob scratched at the underside of his chin. Since she'd mentioned she'd liked his beard, he'd been letting it grow in again.

He was the perfect level of scruffiness.

"We're going to track down this tunnel and Dryden. I'll get the guys." He leaned forward and studied her. "I hate to ask this…"

He didn't have to ask. "You want me to stay here, and not join in the search. Not because you fault my skills or for some he-man need to protect your woman, but because I will actually slow everyone down and split your focus." Like Jacko had said earlier, no offense taken. She was slower these days, and not up to punishing hikes and searches—yet. She'd get there.

"No, it's totally a he-man thing. I want to do this for you, and I want to protect you." Oddjob grinned, absolutely unabashed at his declaration. "I *need* to do this. To know these bastards aren't going to hurt you again directly or indirectly."

"Not going to make you fight me over it," she told him. "I've got work here, I can put myself in lockdown in the house." She was slow, not helpless or stupid.

"Woman, you rock my world. I'll call the guys and get started on a grid search." He rose, then circled the desk. Turning, she met his kiss with one of her own.

"One condition," she told him, gripping his shirt.

"Name it."

"You come back in one piece." She'd just found him.

"I just found you," he said, echoing her thought. "You aren't rid of me that easily."

"Good." Another kiss, and then he was gone, a man on a mission. She almost felt sorry for the people responsible.

Almost.

CHAPTER 8

ONCE ODDJOB ALERT HANK, the Brotherhood lead made a call. Two hours later, Oddjob joined the guys as they dropped in on an open tunnel mine north of Celebrate. It was on public land, tucked behind trees into a hillside. A helicopter pilot friend of Hank's tracked the location for them. A well-used road through the trees allowed access to the roads, via a state highway.

"We're waiting for the sheriff," Hank said over comms as they took their positions. "This is public land, which means we can't nail them for trespassing but it's also up to the state and the local officials to deal with it."

"We're just backing them up," Swede replied.

"Sure, we're here to keep an eye out, civic duty." Bear's rumbling voice carried only a hint of humor.

None of them were happy with the situation, least of all Oddjob. Movement around the mine suggested people were working inside, but only one huge truck was parked at near the opening where the rail let out. So they had mine carts. It was a little too old style Looney Tunes for Oddjob.

He'd found a good spot to watch both the road and the opening. They could dig in and wait for as long as it took. Mickey remained back at Celebrate, and would continue to patrol the ranch. Just because they thought they located the possible source, no one wanted to take any chances.

"Some days I miss running the operation remote and off the grid where we were there to do the mission and get out." Sometimes. He'd never run an op where one of the collateral could be the woman he was falling in love with.

The thought jolted him.

"Sometimes," Flint agreed, and others echoed. "Then I remember where I get to sleep at night and I wish we could have confirmation to leave these guys gift wrapped for the law."

Soft laughter greeted the comment. The sheriff, however, took his time. Likely making sure he had his T's crossed and his i's dotted. Oddjob relied on his training, but Shayna was never far from his thoughts.

In love.

His grandmother's deep laugh echoed through his memory. She'd have enjoyed the hell out of the story about how he realized what he felt for Shayna while in the middle of an op. She would have adored Shayna, too.

When the sheriff arrived, however, he descended

with state troopers and park rangers. Apparently, they were not only on public land—but venturing under the state parks as well as private property.

The raid was anticlimactic, a dozen men rounded up swiftly and the teams broke off to explore the mine itself.

Despite the ease or maybe because of it, Oddjob couldn't settle. They had to wait to identify each of the men currently handcuffed and sitting in a row. The park rangers took control of the site, while the State Troopers called in transport for the arrestees.

"What's eating you?" Hank asked.

"Which one of those guys is Dryden?" Was the real estate buyer a part of this? Or just a dupe involved in picking up the land?

"Checking," Flint said over comms. They'd left them open. Meanwhile Swede and Bear were still sweeping a mine which stretched a couple of miles... directly below Celebrate and along the border separating her land from the neighbor's. After a moment, Flint looked over to them and shook his head.

"We don't know how involved he is," Hank said. "We'll get it sorted."

Yeah, they would. But when?

"We've got a sign of a cave in here, looks like it matches the coordinates for the cabin on Shayna's property. I'm going to guess based on the way they were blasting down here, they hit a gas pocket."

A gas pocket.

So the explosion was an accident.

"We're rerouting down another tunnel, it angles

away, but I'm going to bet that second cabin caught the same way." Swede didn't add anything else, but he didn't have to.

"An accident doesn't explain the vandalism." Hank said.

That was it. "Blasting wouldn't have tampered with her jeep brakes, either." He pushed away from sheriff's car. "I'm getting back to her. If they were after the land, they may have thought she was a squatter or something. Maybe an accident was easier than an offer."

"Dalton told them no," Hank said, looking at his phone. "Sadie just talked to Jacob. He got an offer a few weeks back, turned them down flat. They made a second offer two days before the vandalism started, he was one his way to a shoot in Budapest, turned that down and said he'd donated the land."

Which mean Shayna was still a target.

"Keep me in the loop," he called, already jogging for his truck they'd parked farther up the road.

"Will do."

He was already dialing Mickey's number as he climbed in the truck. When he got voicemail, he said, "Check on Shayna. We got the mine locked down but Dryden wasn't here and I have a bad feeling about this." After hanging up the call, he got the engine started, and backed all the way to the road. He didn't have time for games. He needed to get back to the ranch, now.

As MUCH AS she tried to work, Shayna couldn't concentrate on numbers with Oddjob and the rest of the Brotherhood out there hunting. Mickey came by the house to let her know he was going to do a circuit on the property. With work proving elusive, she headed out to the kitchen and she'd begun compiling the ingredients to start a stew when the sound of a vehicle outside caught her attention.

Wiping her hands on a towel, she walked to the window and checked. A man she didn't recognize exited an expensive Lincoln. Dressed in a suit and bearing a briefcase, he had the look of a businessman. She made it the door a moment before he knocked.

"Can I help you?" Not bothering to open the door wide, she studied the man in front of her. Sweat dotted his brow which also seemed permanently set in a frown.

"I'm here on behalf of Jacob Dalton," he said, a hint of hesitation in his voice and his gaze darted past her.

"Tell you what, why don't you give me your card and I'll call Mr. Dalton and verify." Something was off with the guy. Years in the field taught her to trust those instincts.

"Of course," he stuttered, a little, but it was there. He half turned as he reached into the inside pocket of his jacket. What he pulled out was a gun, not a card and she backed off from the door as he thrust his arm through.

Idiot.

Slamming the door against his arm, he squeezed off a shot that hit a window across the room—shattering the glass. Leaning all her weight into the door, she managed to get the gun out of his hand as he screamed.

Ripping the door open, she ignored the heat from the muzzle as she gripped the body of the gun and whacked him in the face. Blood sprouted from his nose, and he dropped the briefcase and lunged at her. Hobbled by her slow leg, she still managed to evade, and dropped herself to the ground sweeping her leg out to trip him.

He went down and she pointed the gun at him.

"Don't move."

Using the wall to inch her way up, she kept the gun trained on him. The familiar sound of Oddjob's truck tearing up the driveway made her smile.

"Dude, you have no idea who you are messing with."

A moment later, Oddjob bounded up the steps and he looked from her to the guy on the ground and back.

"Hope you don't mind," she said with a relieved grin. "I couldn't sit this part out."

Laughing, he grabbed her would be attacker off the ground and hauled him to his feet. "Oorah."

Four weeks later...

Shayna limped out to the verandah to watch the sun rise. Cradling a hot cup of coffee in her hand, she blew out a breath. It was going to be a great day. Paul Dryden was sitting in jail, his bail denied. The copper mine had been shutdown, and since the deposits were under Celebrate and her neighbor, it had been sealed. They weren't interested in the byproducts of mining —like accidentally blowing up cabins or poisoning the water.

Dryden hadn't confessed to tampering with her brakes, but one of the men who worked for him implicated him in the order. There were a lot of legal hoops to jump through. She'd take them, one at a time. For now, Celebrate was going to be welcoming their first residents that afternoon and she'd found a sponsor for the greenhouse. They'd be breaking ground on that sometime the following month.

A floorboard squeaked, and a moment later, Oddjob wrapped his arms around her. "Good morning," he said, his voice thick with sleep. He smelled fantastic.

"Good morning," she smiled, and held up her coffee cup so he could have a drink.

"Hmm, I think I love you," he murmured, nuzzling her head before taking the cup.

"I know I love you," she told him. The words were remarkably easy to say. He squeezed her middle and handed back the cup.

"This is my favorite part of the day," he told her. "Waking up, and facing the new day with you."

"You're staying." It wasn't a question.

"I told you, when I commit—I'm here for the long haul."

Yes, yes he had. "Fergus," she tried out his name and they both paused. When she laughed, he chuckled.

"Oddjob, babe. Just call me Oddjob."

"At least until I meet your mom, she might object."

"Nah," he told her, as she leaned into him. The sun light spilling across the horizon brightening by the moment. "She's going to love you, because I do."

Shayna hoped so. "This is my new normal," she said. "You. Me. And every day—one sunrise a time."

"Oorah," he whispered against her ear and she grinned. He would never forget she was a Marine, and he wouldn't let her forget either.

Hell yeah, oorah.

Her Marine Bodyguard

Bravo Team Wolf
When Danger Bites
Bitten Under Fire

Boomers
The Judas Contact
Deadly Genesis
Unstoppable

Chance Monroe

Earth Witches Aren't Easy
Plan Witch from Out of Town
Bad Witch Rising

Elite Metal

Pure Copper (Elite Metal)
Target: Tungsten (Elite Ghosts)
Asset: Arsenic (Elite Elements)

Fevered Hearts

Marshal of Hel Dorado
Brave are the Lonely
Micah & Mrs. Miller
A Fistful of Dreams

Raising Kane

Wanted: Fevered or Alive

Wild and Fevered

The Quick & The Fevered

A Man Called Wyatt

Going Royal

Some Like It Royal

Some Like It Scandalous

Some Like It Deadly

Some Like it Secret

Some Like it Easy

Her Marine Prince

Blocked

Lone Star Leathernecks

Semper Fi Cowboy

As You Were Cowboy

Magic & Mayhem

The Witch Singer

Bridget's Witch's Diary

The Witched Away Bride

Every Witch Way But Floosey's

Mongrels

Mongrels, Mischief & Mayhem

Space Cowboy

Space Cowboy Survival Guide

Showdown at the Omega Kilo Space Station

Special Forces Operation Alpha/Brotherhood Protectors

Securing Arizona

Chasing Katie

Guarding Gertrude

Protecting Pilar

Wrangling Wanda

Shielding Shayna

Covering Coco

Wolves of Willow Bend

Wolf at Law

Wolf Bite

Caged Wolf

Wolf Claim

Wolf Next Door

Rogue Wolf

Bayou Wolf

Untamed Wolf

Wolf with Benefits

River Wolf

Single Wicked Wolf

Desert Wolf

Snow Wolf

Wolf on Board

Holly Jolly Wolf

Shadow Wolf

His Moonstruck Wolf

Thunder Wolf

Ghost Wolf

ORIGINAL BROTHERHOOD PROTECTORS SERIES

BY ELLE JAMES

ABOUT ELLE JAMES

ELLE JAMES also writing as MYLA JACKSON is a *New York Times* and *USA Today* Bestselling author of books including cowboys, intrigues and paranormal adventures that keep her readers on the edges of their seats. With over eighty works in a variety of sub-genres and lengths she has published with Harlequin, Samhain, Ellora's Cave, Kensington, Cleis Press, and Avon. When she's not at her computer, she's traveling, snow skiing, boating, or riding her ATV, dreaming up new stories. Learn more about Elle James at www.ellejames.com

Website | Facebook | Twitter | GoodReads | Newsletter | BookBub | Amazon

Follow Elle!
www.ellejames.com
ellejames@ellejames.com

www.ingramcontent.com/pod-product-compliance
Lightning Source LLC
Chambersburg PA
CBHW060640130626
46555CB00002B/892

* 9 7 8 1 6 2 6 9 5 1 6 1 7 *